Praise for Cat Johnson's
Unridden

"Fans of Cat Johnson prepare for her to unlock your deepest desires with this memorable story!"

~ *The Romance Studio*

"...adventurous, passionate and very, very stirring."

~ *Just Erotic Romance Reviews*

"...a pleasure to read. The bullriding scenes were right on and the sex scenes, well......they were, too! ... Ms. Johnson does know her cowboys!"

~ *PNR Reviews*

"Slade and Mustang really captured my heart... it's nearly impossible for any woman to resist them."

~ *Romance Junkies*

"Cat Johnson has delivered another ménage to swoon for in Unridden... You have the angst, the tension, and oodles of white hot sex."

~ *Whipped Cream Reviews*

Look for these titles by *Cat Johnson*

Now Available:

Rough Stock

Studs in Spurs Series
Unridden (Book 1)
Bucked (Book 2)

Red, Hot and Blue Series
Trey (Book 1)
Jack (Book 2)

Unridden

Cat Johnson

A Samhain Publishing, Ltd. publication.

Samhain Publishing, Ltd.
577 Mulberry Street, Suite 1520
Macon, GA 31201
www.samhainpublishing.com

Editing by Heidi Moore
Cover by Amanda Kelsey

This book has been previously published.
First Samhain Publishing, Ltd. electronic publication: November 2009
First Samhain Publishing, Ltd. print publication: September 2010

Dedication

For Mike Short, the bull-riding cowboy who took the time to help me write this and came up with the original (or maybe not so original) idea of a romance writer who meets a cowboy while researching her book. Any liberties taken or mistakes made with the facts are purely my own.

Prologue

"So? What did you think?"

Much like an accused man watches the faces of the jury returning with a verdict, Jenna Block held her breath as she studied her literary agent's expression.

Marge Collins of the Collins Agency had a reputation for not pulling any punches. Swallowing hard, Jenna guessed Marge's tightly pursed lips and hesitation were not good signs. She had a feeling her delicate writer's ego was about to get a lesson in humility.

The manuscript sat on the desk between them like an eight-hundred-pound gorilla. Her agent sighed. Another bad sign.

Suddenly feeling like a child seated in front of the wide desk, Jenna straightened her spine. Was her chair lower than Marge's? That sneaky, power-grabbing ploy on the part of her agent wouldn't surprise Jenna one little bit.

Marge peered over top of her reading glasses. "Jenna, there's really no market for straight contemporaries right now."

Jenna frowned, confused. She'd assumed the sale of this book would be a slam dunk.

"There was a market last year when you sold my last straight contemporary. In fact, you had no trouble selling my last three novels."

Marge nodded. "You're right, but the trend in the industry has shifted."

"In under a year?"

"That's why it's called a trend, I guess." She shrugged.

Biting her lower lip, Jenna tried to digest the idea of totally scrapping the novel she'd spent a considerable portion of the last year writing and starting fresh with a new one. In a different genre, no less. The thought had her stomach twisting with dread. How in the world was she going to write a new book and get it sold before this apparently fickle and ever-changing romance market shifted yet again?

Hesitantly, Jenna asked, "What's the new trend?" *Please don't say historical romance.* She absolutely loathed research, which was one reason why she wrote only contemporaries.

Marge leaned back and steepled her fingers. "The publishers want cross-genre, out-of-the-box stories."

What the hell did that mean? Panicked, Jenna did her best to keep her expression neutral. "Okay, like what for example?"

"Well, I just sold an erotic, multi-partner, paranormal romance with elements of bondage about pirate vampires in space." Marge waited expectantly, as if Jenna would leap up and say that she had written a book just like that and had it stashed under her bed.

Jenna sat perfectly still, hoping her face didn't show her horror. Bondage issue aside—how did one research *that* subject—her brain stalled on visions of her brother hiding the remote control and making her watch agonizing hours of the SyFy Channel on television when they were kids.

Science fiction. Ugh. Was she destined to now spend her days penning tales of horny vampire space pirates?

Jenna swallowed the ever-growing lump in her throat. "Um, anything else selling?"

Marge shuffled a few pages on the desk. "There is a publisher who put out an open call for submissions for their new cowboy line of romances."

Cowboys. Okay, she could do cowboys.

"Space pirate cowboys?" Jenna asked with probably a bit more attitude than was wise considering her writing career and the fate of her future manuscripts were in this woman's hands.

Eyes narrowed, Marge pursed her lips but answered her anyway. "No. Regular cowboys."

"Contemporary or historical?" Jenna could fake knowing about modern cowboys. She'd just have them wear jeans and boots and chew on a piece of hay or spit tobacco or something. However, writing about the Old West would require actual research. Even if Jenna had the desire, she didn't have the time for that. A writer was only as good as her most recent book and too much time had already passed since her last release.

Marge finally ended Jenna's suspense. "Any genre is fine, so long as it has a cowboy theme."

That was good news at least. Still overwhelmed by the idea of starting over from scratch, Jenna let out a sigh. "When's the deadline for submissions?"

Marge glanced down at the paper in her hand and cringed. "A month and a half from now."

"A month and a half?"

"Can you do that?" Marge raised one eyebrow dubiously.

With a romance convention coming up out west, book signings scheduled, on top of radio interviews and a virtual tour online to various chats and blogs, Jenna had countless other things to do over the next few weeks besides plotting out and completing this new book. She wasn't a slow writer, but she wasn't super fast by any means. "What length are they looking for?"

Again, Marge consulted the paper that had delivered more bad than good news so far. "They want between fifty and sixty thousand words. And they're looking for stories that are fun and light in tone."

Jenna snorted out a laugh. "Fifty thousand words in a month and a half on top of everything else I have going on? It's going to be light. Don't worry about that." She sure as hell didn't have time to do heavy, though she doubted anything about this would be fun.

Rising from her seat, Jenna let out an overly loud breath. "I guess I better go home and get started."

There went her plans for some retail therapy in the stores while she was in the city for the day. She would have to hop right on the next train and get back to her laptop at her condo in the suburbs.

Marge pushed Jenna's manuscript across the desk. "Don't forget this."

Jenna eyed the sheaf of papers with sudden, undeserved hatred. "Don't you want to keep it, just in case?"

"I guess I could try to dump it on one of the smaller, indie e-publishers. Most of them don't pay advances, but it's better than nothing. Send me the electronic file when you get home and I'll see what I can do."

Dump it. Great.

Jenna forced a tight and far–from-sincere smile. "Thanks, Marge. You're a sweetheart."

"No problem, Jen. See you in six weeks."

Marge slid her glasses back up her nose and turned her attention to the next stack of papers on her cluttered desk. Apparently, Jenna had been dismissed. Stifling a groan, she mumbled a goodbye and gladly retreated from the office.

Chapter One

"Slade Bower needs an eighty-nine to take the lead in this competition. What do you think, folks? Can Slade do it? He's riding One-Night Stand from Double J Stock Contractors. Tonight is this bull's first time out in this series. Since we've never seen him before, there's no telling how he's gonna come out of the chute. Slade's definitely at a disadvantage in this match up."

On the edge of his consciousness, Slade could hear the arena announcer's amplified ramblings. The steady chatter entertained the crowd in the stands while Slade concentrated on getting himself properly seated on the bull's broad back. Meanwhile, the beast did everything it could to make that difficult for him.

Even though it was this animal's first time out in big time competition, the damn bull somehow already knew a few of the tricks pulled by the veteran stock. Slade tried getting his denim and leather-covered leg into position but the bull countered by leaning all his weight against the back rails of the bucking chute to make sure the cowboy it didn't want on its back couldn't wiggle his leg down.

Slade saw a booted foot swing over the top rail of the chute and brace against the animal's side. His friend, Mustang Jackson, was trying to help by pushing the bull away from the wall. Slade quickly slid his leg down into the small space

Mustang had created for him while the bull tried to lean again and crush him.

The bull had already bucked once in the chute when one of the guys tightened the rope that stretched beneath One-Night Stand's belly so Slade could wrap it around his left hand. He wasn't going to wait around for the animal to pitch a fit in the chute again. Surrounded by metal in an incredibly tight space with a couple thousand pounds of bucking bull was a good way to get knocked out cold or worse before the ride even began.

Enough with the bullshit. Time to get the show started. Slade settled his ass one final time on the bull's back and gave a nod. The gate swung open and One-Night Stand bolted out of the chute, starting to buck before his flank even cleared the metal rail.

The bull took off, circling to the left and into Slade's riding hand, before reversing and rounding to the right. Slade felt his body slide to one side after the reversal but made the correction, readjusting and centering his weight.

No longer aware of the announcer or much of anything, Slade engaged in a battle of wills and wits with the two thousand pounds of bucking animal beneath him. His field of vision narrowed to a small area between the bull's shoulder blades. Keeping his toes turned out and his spurs pressed against the animal's hide, Slade held on tight as One-Night Stand gave him one hell of a ride.

The animal was smart and strong. When Slade's weight slipped to one side, the bull snapped around fast and bucked hard in the opposite direction, trying anything to get the rider off its back. Unfortunately for the bull, Slade was just as smart and a hell of a lot more stubborn as he made countless corrections to his position and used all of his strength to keep himself forward and up on top of his rope.

The odds were good for Slade to make the eight seconds, until the cunning animal dipped its front end low, then whipped back up, sharp and fast, nearly causing Slade to kiss the back of its big, bony head.

Pulling his torso backwards, Slade tried not to slap the bull with his free hand. That would end the ride for him instantly. If Slade got bucked off, so be it, but he'd be damned before he'd get disqualified for a slap. The judges could and would do that to him for breaking the rules if his right hand touched either the animal or himself.

He managed to keep his free hand up and clear, but the bull's move got Slade leaned back too far onto his pockets and his left hand slipped free of the rope wrapped around his glove.

Slade was airborne just as the buzzer sounded above the noise of the crowd.

The bullfighters moved in immediately to distract the still-bucking animal as Slade landed on his shoulder with a grunt and then rolled clear of the deadly hooves that pounded the ground inches from his face.

Jumping to his feet, he got to the relative safety of the rails before locating the scoreboard, not sure if he'd made the full eight seconds. The first of the four judges' scores appeared on the monitor and Slade punched the air in victory. He'd done it. Ridden One-Night Stand right down to the buzzer. Barely.

The announcer's voice reverberated throughout the arena, "Ninety point five is the score. With only one rider left tonight to challenge his position, Slade Bower takes the lead."

The bull ran for the gate leading to the stock pens and disappeared out of the arena. Slade grinned, high-fiving one of the bullfighters.

"Great ride, Slade." Another of the bullfighters congratulated him and handed him the rope that had fallen off the bull moments after Slade had.

Slade took his bull rope and then pulled the mouthpiece from between his teeth, stashing it in a pocket. "Thanks, Shorty."

The fringe of Slade's leather chaps swished, slapping his legs as he strode from the arena and headed behind the bucking chutes. He flipped his rope over a railing and turned back to watch the action in the chute where his competition, the one rider who could cost him the win tonight, was about to ride.

"Hey, man. Great ride."

Eyes still trained on the rider straddling the rails over the bull in the chute, Slade accepted a congratulatory slap on the back from Mustang. "Thanks, man." He ripped open the Velcro closure before unzipping his logo-covered protective vest.

His friend cleared his throat. "Uh, Slade?"

"Yeah?" Slade kept his gaze on the rider getting settled on the bull.

"I got something for ya."

Frowning at the interruption, Slade turned toward Mustang, and was confronted by a lacy pair of red panties dangling from his friend's forefinger.

"Jesus, Mustang." Slade grabbed the embarrassing garment and stuffed it inside his vest as he glanced around for any television cameras that might have caught Mustang's incredible lack of good judgment. "Where the hell did you get these?"

"From that hot number who was giving us the eye from the stands earlier."

Slade raised a brow and, good and distracted now, was barely aware of the gate opening as the next and final matchup of the night began. "You mean the one with the tits?"

A huge kid-on-Christmas-morning grin lit Mustang's face. "Yup. That's the one."

Slade blew out a long, slow breath. He noticed the rider in the arena get a face full of dirt a full two seconds before the buzzer. His win now secure, he could concentrate on other things. "She got a friend?"

"She does, but the word is her friend is currently passed out in their car after decorating the floor of the ladies' room with some bourbon-soaked french fries." Slade cringed at that too-vivid description. "But no sweat, I am perfectly willing to share, 'cause that's the kind of guy I am."

Slade rolled his eyes at Mustang's false generosity. The two of them shared women more often than not. "She's cool with that? You know...both of us?"

"Oh, yeah. In fact, she's really into it. Or at least that's the impression I got when she asked if me and my tall, dark and handsome friend—which I guess meant you—wanted to make a cowgirl sandwich with her after the competition was over." Mustang grinned wider, if possible.

"A cowgirl sandwich? She did not seriously say that."

"Hell yeah, she did."

Slade ran the tip of his tongue slowly over his teeth in anticipation. "All right then. Let me go collect my paycheck and I'll meet you in the trailer."

"The trailer." Mustang shook his head and snorted out a loud puff of air. "I can't believe all the hotels nearby were sold out for that college homecoming game except for one that you refuse to stay in because it costs too much. Whoever is in charge of choosing the dates and locations for this series should

17

check things like that out. We end up sleeping in that trailer too damn much for my liking."

Even though Slade was walking away with a damn nice paycheck for tonight's win, there was no way he would willingly spend three hundred and fifty bucks for a bed for one night, especially when Mustang had a perfectly nice trailer. Besides, they were both always one ride away from an injury that could take them out of competition for months, if not forever. It was smart not to squander money on things like three-hundred-and-fifty-dollar-a-night hotel rooms. A bed was a bed. Who cared if it was in a trailer or some fancy hotel?

There was one other reason Slade preferred to not sleep in a hotel. "I like staying in the trailer. It's always easier to get women to leave right away after we're done with them. They tend to hang around too long if the hotel room is too nice."

Rolling his eyes, Mustang pushed his cowboy hat back with one finger. "You are the biggest commitment-phobe I've ever seen. Just 'cause they stay the night doesn't mean you have to marry them. Besides, I happen to really like morning sex, something I don't get to enjoy lately with you kicking them out the minute you're done."

"Whatever," Slade grumbled. "I'll meet you in the trailer in a few."

"Yeah, yeah. See you in the trailer."

With that, Mustang left to retrieve the makings for their sandwich, leaving Slade with visions of the pleasures that were to come. He pivoted on the heel of one boot and headed to smile big for the cameras and get his even bigger check.

Tucking the red panties deeper beneath his vest, he gave the quickest interview of his life to the reporter, smiled and then accepted the giant cardboard check as the flashbulbs clicked around him. The press done, he grabbed his rope from the railing, stowed it in his gear bag with the rest of his stuff and whistled the entire way to the trailer and the well-endowed hot number that awaited him there.

It was good to know that in this world of deception the girl from the arena hadn't done any false advertising when she'd strutted in wearing painted-on blue jeans and a shirt that left nothing to the imagination. When Slade swung open the door of the trailer he came face-to-face with a gorgeous, heart-shaped, naked ass decorated with a butterfly tattoo.

The girl didn't waste any time. He liked that in a lay.

The owner of the artful ass was currently on the bed on her knees, tits swaying as she rocked over Mustang, whose cock was already buried in her throat. She held it with both fists and struggled to take in the whole thing. There was a reason the man was called Mustang, and it had nothing to do with the model of car.

With a grin at his friend, Slade slammed and locked the door. He dropped his gear bag on the floor and began stripping out of his chaps. It didn't take long to fling off his vest, shirt, boots and jeans. Soon, still wearing his hat, he knelt on the bed behind the girl.

Mustang flipped him a strip of condoms and Slade caught it one-handed. He tore into the foil with his teeth and rolled one on, for disease prevention as well as a fear of pregnancy. He didn't want to deal with a possible paternity lawsuit now his career had taken off.

Hell, if he never saw this woman again, that would be fine with him. They'd enjoy tonight and then he and Mustang would take off tomorrow for the next city in the lineup of competitions. But Slade was sure they'd leave this little cowgirl with some damn good memories after they'd gone.

One dip of a finger inside her told Slade she was more than ready for him. Anchoring her with a hand on each shapely hip, he plunged inside with one good, hard thrust.

The adrenaline of the ride never dissipated right away. He was keyed up and usually hard enough to cut diamonds after each and every competition. Thankfully, there were always plenty of women waiting in the wings to help him out.

Slade pounded into the girl, not worrying about technique or much anything else. His goal was to release the tension built up inside him so he could relax and sink deep into the mellow feeling his body succumbed to after the adrenaline rush subsided.

Focused on the butterfly inked just above the crack of the jiggling ass in front of him, Slade increased his speed until he heard Mustang draw in a hiss of a breath. "Watch the teeth, darlin'. That there is precious cargo in your mouth."

Slade couldn't control his laugh at his friend's comment. "I'll be done in a sec. Then she's all yours."

There was no reason to prolong it. He wasn't really into this tonight, except for the release it would provide him. Closing his eyes, Slade's hands tightened on... Damn, he didn't even know her name. That fact made no difference.

With his eyes shut, Slade could forget she was just another random woman he'd never see again. It didn't matter he didn't know her name, or that tomorrow morning he'd wake up alone in the trailer with nothing but Mustang's snoring to disturb him. He'd be grateful for that because the last thing he wanted was to see this faceless, nameless woman again. Not that there would be fear of seeing her again. Tomorrow they'd be in another town.

He plunged in one last time, held deep and came with quick, powerful spurts.

After one final shudder, Slade pulled out. He dealt with the condom and then flung himself into the chair right next to the largest bed in the crowded trailer. Through heavily lidded eyes, he watched the rest of the show.

Mustang tore open a condom for himself before saying, "Hop on up here, darlin'. Let's see if you can handle the ride."

"I can handle it. Don't you worry." Eyes watery from being nearly gagged by Mustang, the girl looked relieved and slightly wobbly as she climbed on top of him. Then she had to struggle to lower herself onto him and her relief disappeared.

"I'm not worried, darlin'. You just take it slow. Ooo wee, that feels good." Hands on her waist, pressing her down onto his cock, Mustang leaned back and grinned at the girl as she labored to accommodate him. "A little farther. Ah. There you go. How's that feel?"

"Good." Her voice sounded breathy. "Real good."

The cowgirl hadn't lied. She could handle Mustang and from the looks of her, she was enjoying it.

Slade shook his head and smiled as he listened to it all from his chair. It always amused him that, unlike himself, Mustang was a talker during sex, continuously reassuring and encouraging the girls with compliments and comments.

Mustang's running sex dialogue probably came from years of having to convince females that his enormous dick would indeed fit inside them if they'd just let him give it a try. Slade was no slouch in the size area himself, but even he had to admit that Mustang deserved his nickname. The man was hung like a horse.

Slade had been there to witness Mustang's powers of verbal persuasion on more than a few occasions. "Just let me put the tip in, darlin'. That's all. I swear," Mustang would coo to the usually skeptical-looking female.

Of course, Mustang would inevitably end up getting his way, even with the most uncertain women and the tightest places.

The one virgin they'd encountered hadn't been immune to Mustang's silver tongue either. It had taken all night, but the "just the tip, darlin'" argument had eventually led to her being a virgin no more. Slade couldn't complain. Mustang was good at sharing. Slade always benefited from his powers of persuasion, but there were times when the things Mustang said to the women they shared were such bullshit, Slade had to cover his mouth to hide his smile.

This proved to be one of those times. Slade nearly laughed out loud now when Mustang said, "I'll remember this night forever, darlin'."

Absently, Slade wondered if Mustang had gotten her name before shoving his dick in her mouth the moment he'd gotten her into the trailer. Not that it really mattered.

Damn. What was up with him tonight? He usually didn't feel so cold about the women they entertained. They were nearing the end of the season. That was probably it. He and Mustang could both use a rest for a few months, not that Mustang seemed to be feeling the same way. He looked like a kid who'd just robbed the candy store as he bounced the cowgirl on his dick.

Slade enjoyed a few more minutes of watching her jostling tits and jiggling ass cheeks before Mustang came with a shout and a curse. The girl flopped over to lie panting on the bed, looking like she'd gotten more than she bargained for when she offered a cowgirl sandwich to two adrenaline-fueled bull riders.

Mustang caught Slade's eye and must have seen his weariness. He rolled toward the cowgirl and propped his head on his hand. "Don't you think you'd better go see to your friend, darlin'? I'm worried about her. I've see people get mighty sick, die even, from alcohol poisoning."

Her eyes opened wide and her face paled. "Oh my God. Do you think she might be..."

"I'm no doctor. I'm just saying there ain't no telling what can happen. I know I'd want to check if it was Slade there alone in a car possibly choking to death on his own vomit."

At that colorful scenario, she flew off the bed to search the trailer for her clothes.

Slade realized she wouldn't find her panties since Mustang had given them to him back in the arena. Nude except for his once white socks and black cowboy hat, Slade rose with some effort and no modesty to retrieve her undies from amid the pile of clothes he'd dropped near the door.

Barely making eye contact, she took them back from him with a mumbled, "Thanks."

"No problem." Pulling up his own underwear, Slade watched as she threw her clothes on. She looked as anxious to get out of there as he was for her to leave now that he was done with her. That realization made him feel strangely sad for both of them.

When the door finally closed behind her, leaving him and Mustang alone, Slade let out a sigh and collapsed back into the chair.

Mustang shot him an unhappy look. "What's up with you tonight?"

"What do you mean?"

"I mean you acting like you could barely muster the energy to fuck an incredibly hot chick."

Slade shrugged. "I don't know. It's just not as fun as it used to be."

Mustang frowned and stared at him as if he'd grown dick antlers. "Fucking isn't as fun as it used to be?"

Slade considered that for a second. "Maybe that's the problem. It's just fucking."

Mustang looked horrified. "So what are you saying, Slade? You want to find a girl, get married, buy a house with a white picket fence and settle down in a nice, boring, safe job? Do you know how much sex married men get from their wives? Next to none, that's how much. Ask Jorge. He'll tell you."

A wife, a real job and a house with a white picket fence? No. Definitely not. A nice farm and a steady girlfriend to go home to between competitions? That didn't sound so bad. Maybe.

Slade kept his surmising to himself. "No, that's not what I'm saying. But it gets old. A different girl each night. Not even knowing their names."

"You may not know their names, but I do." After pulling on his boxers, Mustang sat forward on the bed and braced his forearms on his knees as he ticked off a list of data for Slade. "She said her name was Brandi, spelled with an 'i'. Just from knowing her for one night I am betting she dots that 'i' with a heart when she writes it. She just graduated from the local community college. Her brother is in the Army in Iraq right now. Her mother thinks cowboys are nothing but trouble, which is most likely why she was here tonight with us. Oh, and she doesn't make a peep when she comes, but she shakes like a leaf stuck in the windshield wiper of a truck speeding down the highway."

Damn. Mustang had done his homework. That made Slade feel even shittier since he'd had no inclination to know anything more about the girl besides that she had what he needed for the few minutes he was inside her. Somehow, that seemed wrong.

"Hmm. I didn't notice her coming," Slade commented for lack of anything else to say.

"That's because I took care of her quick before you got here."

"Oh. Good." He felt a little better knowing that.

Where the hell was this pall coming from?

Slade was usually happy to just fuck and relax. This self-analysis and introspection wasn't like him at all. "I'm glad you got to know her a bit, anyway."

"I didn't ask questions and listen to her answers because of some sudden sexual guilt like you seem to be suffering from." Mustang dismissed Slade's comment with a snort and a wave of his hand. "You know damn well I like flirting with the pretty girls. When I noticed her watching us from the stands, I knew all it would take was a little bit of buttering her up to get her into bed. You should be damned grateful I do like the buttering up part since by the end of the competition she was offering herself up to both of us like a cowgirl sandwich on a silver platter, pretty red panties and all."

Mustang grinned at his own description, while Slade pressed his lips together and drew in a deep breath through his nose. "I guess I haven't been pulling my weight in the buttering up department. Sorry."

Mustang looked disgusted, further raising Slade's level of annoyance as he defended himself. "What? Damn it, Mustang. I said I'm sorry. Next woman, I'll reel in. Okay?"

"That's not the problem. The hunt is the fun part for me, well, second to fucking. But you won the competition tonight and got laid, and you didn't even have to talk to the girl to do it. So why do you seem so damned depressed? You're starting to make me worry about you."

Slade sighed and considered the question carefully. "Hell. I don't know, Mustang. I guess I'm bored."

"Bored? Well, okay then. *That* at least I can understand. Next time we'll get us a couple of girls. Two, or three even. Maybe we should stop at the next sex shop we see and pick up some toys. One of those vibrating ones. Girls like those. We're running low on lube anyway."

"Okay. Sounds good." Even in his crappy mood, Slade had to smile at Mustang's newest ideas for their extracurricular activities.

Visions of the girl they'd had last week and vivid memories of what they'd done to her, the reason they were almost out of lube, flitted through his head. That had been one woman they, or rather Mustang, didn't have to persuade. She hadn't even batted an eye at the size of Mustang's dick, or his suggestions as to where inside her it would fit nicely. It took half a tube of lube, but Slade was a witness that it had indeed fit perfectly.

Mustang grinned and rose from the bed, slapping Slade on the shoulder. "This too shall pass, my friend. You're looking happier already. I'm heading for a shower."

Slade nodded. A shower, a solid night's sleep and then the open road and it would all be good. By the next city he'd have shaken this mood and be back in action.

"Mustang," he called loud enough for his friend to hear over the sound of the running water.

"Yeah?"

"Keep your eye out in the audience for twins. I've always wanted to have me some twins."

Slade heard Mustang's loud laugh through the door of the bathroom and grinned. He felt lighter already.

Chapter Two

"Does that horse have horns?" Jenna's best friend, Astrid, squinted at something over Jenna's shoulder.

"What?" She had a few better questions than that. First and foremost, why the hell had Astrid insisted the two of them come to a sports bar, the male equivalent of Disneyland, for girl's night out? Just as importantly, why didn't Astrid give in and get glasses or contact lenses so she could actually see without squinting? Jenna hated to think how the woman was able to drive and read street signs with her vision.

With a sigh of resolution, Jenna twisted in her seat to see what Astrid was talking about. She caught a glimpse of one of the two dozen or so television screens adorning the neon-covered walls. "That's not a horse, silly. It's a bull."

Born and raised a suburbanite, Jenna had never actually met a bull in person, but she'd seen them on that television commercial—the one for cheese featuring the boy and girl talking cows.

"A bull? That's crazy. Who would get on top of a bull and try to ride it? Besides, I thought cowboys rode horses." Astrid shook her head, sending her short black hair swinging around her face. The blue highlights she'd recently added picked up the light of the beer sign behind her. One day Astrid would realize that a woman over thirty shouldn't have blue hair.

Jenna angled herself to better see the television now that she knew a rodeo was on. Where there was a rodeo, there must be cowboys, right? At the moment, Jenna needed a good cowboy or two.

Absently, she chewed on the straw in her vodka and cranberry. "Did I tell you I'm writing a cowboy romance now?"

Astrid nearly choked on her light beer. "Really? How are you going to do that? The closest you've come to a cowboy was the guy in the big hat that bumped into you in Grand Central Station last December. Remember, when we went to see the Christmas tree lighting at Rockefeller Center?"

Jenna shrugged as she watched the rider on the television get thrown off the bull, cowboy hat and all, and miss being stepped on by the deadly looking animal by mere inches. The station cut to the commentators in the booth, whom she couldn't hear, so she turned back to answer Astrid. "I just started the book, but I figure it can't be that hard. I mean, really, how complicated can cowboys be? I'll just have him ride around on a horse a lot."

Astrid eyed her suspiciously. "You don't even own a house pet. What in the world do you know about horses?"

"At least I know they don't have horns."

Astrid shot Jenna a nasty look.

Truth be told, Jenna couldn't even keep her houseplants alive, much less an animal, but that wasn't the point. "Besides, I'll research," Jenna continued.

"Research cowboys and horses? How?"

"The Internet. The library. I watched some equestrian competition on ESPN the other day. Cute outfits, by the way. Very vintage Ralph Lauren with the slim pants, high boots and velvet coats. I hope that style comes back in fashion. I really liked it the first time around."

Astrid frowned. "That all doesn't sound very western."

"I was watching to learn about horses. I mean horses are horses. Right? It doesn't matter whether you ride them while you're wearing denim or velvet. It's not the horse part I'm worried about. The problem is I'm having trouble coming up with a good plot for the storyline. My hero keeps sounding too 'Aw shucks, ma'am' for me. If I don't even like the hero, how can I expect my reader to?"

Eyes once again glued to the cowboy action on the television, Astrid slowly traced the tip of one finger through the condensation on her bottle. "You should have your hero be a rodeo cowboy. These guys are sexy. Risking death by riding that big, nasty bull. And mmm mmm, look at those leather chaps. I bet they'd look good with no jeans underneath."

Astrid's bawdy observations aside, Jenna considered the suggestion.

"Hmm. A rodeo cowboy. You might be on to something. All that risk would add to the tension in the story." Jenna searched for a pen in her cluttered purse and then grabbed a cocktail napkin from the stack on the bar to take notes. "Ooo! What about this? His name could be Buck Wild. Get it? Because he rides bucking bulls, and that could be the name of the book too. What do you think?"

Astrid laughed. "I think it sounds like a typical trashy romance novel. So yeah, it's perfect."

Ignoring the "trashy" comment, Jenna wrote the title idea down then glanced back at the television as another man hit the ground hard and still jumped up smiling. These guys were obviously all insane, but Astrid was right, they were also sexy as hell.

Behind the bar, the bartender's smirk and the steady sway of his head drew Jenna's attention away from the television screen. He'd been working the length of the bar the entire time they'd been there. Admittedly, Jenna had sized him up when he'd been too busy to notice. She'd admired the view from head to boot and everything in between, but now the tables were turned. He was watching her and she didn't like it one bit.

She frowned. "Something wrong?"

"No, ma'am. Not a thing." His voice oozed out as slow and smooth as molasses. And his "ma'am"... The dialogue from her book was coming to life right in front of her.

Eyes wide, Jenna leaned forward at the sound of his deep drawl and what it meant to her and the possible future of this book. She saw Astrid raise an interested brow as she also noted his accent.

Jenna considered his western-style shirt, denim jeans and cowboy boots with new interest. Before she'd heard him talk, she had assumed it was some sort of costume required for the bar staff or something.

"Where are you from?" It came out sounding more like an accusation than a question.

"Not from here." He grabbed another dripping glass from the rack he'd been emptying for the last few minutes and dried it with a tattered, white towel. Across the bar he placed the glass with the others.

Jenna wasn't about to be dissuaded so easily by his evasive answer. "Yeah, I gathered that. So where exactly are you from?"

He smirked but made no move to end Jenna's suspense.

"Texas," a cocktail waitress answered for him, to the cowboy's obvious chagrin, before she added, "And I need another pitcher of beer with three cold mugs."

The unhappy Texan went to fill the pitcher, and Jenna took the opportunity to question the waitress further. "He doesn't happen to know anything about rodeos, does he?"

The waitress cackled. "Him? Nah. Don't think so. The word is he used to work on the oil rigs."

"Oh. Okay. Thanks." Jenna's heart fell. Oil rigs. She knew even less about them than horses. Giving her fictional cowboy that profession was out, particularly in light of the Texan bartender's lack of helpfulness so far.

The cowboy returned with the waitress' order, grinning. "Sorry, darlin'. Not all cowboys ride bulls, or even horses for that matter."

With a long look that devoured the man with her eyes, Astrid jumped into the conversation. "You must know something about the rodeo. I mean there are lots of bulls and horses in Texas, right?"

He laughed, a low, rumbling sound. Jenna stifled a groan and watched her friend melt a little bit more over him. The reason Astrid had planned girl's night out in this testosterone pit was becoming quite apparent. She was on the prowl tonight.

"I'm sure I know more than the two of you ladies, but no, I don't know enough to have her quoting me on her little white napkin there." He hooked a thumb in the direction of Jenna and her pen, which was poised and ready for action above the aforementioned cocktail napkin.

Criticism of her research style aside, Jenna decided if he knew anything about rodeo, it would be better than what she knew, which was nothing. "What's your name?"

"Tex."

She raised a brow. "Seriously?"

"Yup." Somehow that one syllable became more like three as he drew it out, long and slow.

"Okay, Tex, I'd be happy to leave you a very generous tip if you'd be willing to give me just a few rodeo details I can use in my book."

As Astrid leaned farther over the bar like a magnet drawn to a big, tall, sexy hunk of metal, Jenna considered throwing her friend into the bargain along with the tip in exchange for some rodeo facts. She was fairly certain Astrid, looking starry-eyed and practically drooling, wouldn't mind.

Tex. Jenna would have to consider naming a side character that. Perhaps Buck Wild could have a best friend.

The man in question pulled a pen from behind his ear, grabbed another cocktail napkin and scribbled something. He shoved it across the bar and went to help a customer.

Astrid slapped one hand down hard onto the bar top and spun to face Jenna. "Oh my God. If he gave you his phone number, I'm going to scream. How come the cute ones always like you best?"

If that were true, then how come Jenna was alone? Very, very alone. Oh yeah, because all men sucked, that's why. Even the tall, dark and Texan ones, she was sure.

Jenna glanced at the napkin in her hand and shook her head. Astrid's hissy fit was for nothing, because all she'd gotten from Tex was one word.

Google.

Hmm, who knew cowboys knew about Internet search engines, even a behemoth like Google? Maybe cowboys weren't as backwoods or backwards as she had thought.

Jenna shoved the napkin at her friend, shot a less than friendly glance in Tex's direction and mumbled, "Smart ass."

Already eyeball-deep into a huge crush, Astrid grinned. "Yeah, he is and I think I like it. Damn, I wish all these people would leave him alone so he'd come back."

So did Jenna, because she still wasn't convinced he hadn't ridden a bull or two himself. If her suspicions were true, she'd get it out of him even if she had to sacrifice Astrid's dubious virtue to do it.

With a sigh, Astrid gave up firing dirty looks at the patrons who were keeping Tex from her and turned back to Jenna. "What do you want to do for your birthday next week?"

Jenna groaned. "Ignore it."

"Oh, come on. It's a milestone. We have to do something."

"Thirty-five is not a milestone." Thirty, yeah, that had been a big one. Forty, God help her, would be even worse. But thirty-five she was willing to ignore. "I'll be away, anyway. Remember?"

Astrid wrinkled her nose, but Jenna wasn't sure if it was related to Tex's persistent absence from their end of the bar, or over Jenna's impending trip during her birthday. "Oh, yeah. I'd forgotten. Where are you going again?"

Jenna rolled her eyes. "A romance writer's conference in Tulsa, Oklahoma, of all places. What the hell could there possibly be to do in Tulsa when we have a break from the convention stuff? It's going to be such a bore."

Aside from the movie *Oklahoma*, which she was pretty sure had also been a musical on Broadway once, she knew nothing about the state except that it was in the middle of the country somewhere and she'd have to suffer through the trip to the airport, security lines and hours in the air to get there.

"Oh my God." Astrid's hand clamped down on Jenna's forearm as she squinted at something over Jenna's shoulder.

"What?"

Astrid was ready to bubble over. "Take a look at the television behind you."

Jenna spun around just in time before the station cut to a commercial to see a graphic on the screen advertising—*oh my*

God was right—next week's bull-riding competition in *Tulsa*. "Holy crap."

She turned back as Astrid grinned. "Looks like you just found something to do in Tulsa next week, and you'll be able to do some rodeo-cowboy research in person at the same time."

Jenna considered her good fortune. It really was serendipity, but one question remained. "What does one wear at a rodeo?"

"How about a cowboy?" Astrid's face shone with an evil grin before she perked up like a dog that had just been shown a bone. "Um, Jen. Don't be mad, but our dates just arrived."

Managing to swallow the sip of her drink she'd just taken instead of choking at that revelation, Jenna set her glass on the bar none too gently. She narrowed her eyes at her supposed friend. "What do you mean our dates?"

"Surprise?" Astrid's smile wavered a bit at Jenna's lack of enthusiasm.

Jenna opened her mouth, about to let Astrid know exactly what she thought of the *surprise*, when she was frantically shushed.

"Shh. Listen. I found them on a matchmaking site online and they're perfect. Just go with it, okay?" Astrid swiveled on her stool to face the two smiling men approaching them.

With a groan, Jenna also turned on her barstool, but to face the bar instead of the two unwelcome dates. She raised her nearly empty glass in the air.

"Another drink please, Tex. Better make it a strong one." Catching one of the guys checking out her ass perched on the stool, Jenna had a feeling she was going to need it.

Chapter Three

Airport security at Newark Liberty International was worse than she remembered, even worse now than it had been immediately after the 9/11 attacks as it felt like new and more stringent restrictions on air travelers were instituted daily. No liquids. No shoes. No coats. By the time Jenna got through the metal detector she was barefoot and practically topless, self-consciously wearing nothing but tight sweatpants and a thin, revealing top that she'd never meant to be seen in public. Unfortunately, she'd forgotten they'd make her remove her zip-up jacket and put it on the conveyor belt along with her shoes and bag.

The Transportation Security Administration guard, who took much less time studying the X-ray image of her carry-on bag than he did her boobs, smiled at her.

Resisting the urge to cross her arms over her chest, Jenna grabbed her belongings as quickly as she could without looking like a terrorist fleeing security. Jenna struggled to locate her now ringing phone in the outside pocket of her bag. With her belongings clutched against her, she padded as quickly as possible away from the security checkpoint. Barefoot still, she made her way to a chair around the corner and out of his line of sight to put her jacket and shoes back on as Astrid's voice came through the phone.

"How's the trip so far?"

Jenna groaned. "I just this minute got through security. And I'm telling you right now, next flight I'm going to wear the wedding band my grandmother left me in her will because I think the TSA guy was just checking me out."

"You got picked up at security? Sometimes I really hate you. Do you know that?"

"Astrid, are you insane?" Jenna still couldn't shake the uncomfortable feeling caused by the agent's roving eyes and Astrid was jealous?

Finally fully covered and more than relieved that the stripping portion of the trip was over, at least for this leg of the journey, Jenna glanced up at the gate numbers and started the walk to hers. Locating her gate not too far down the row, she settled into an empty vinyl chair for the hour plus wait until her flight boarded.

Still sounding unhappy, Astrid went on anyway. "Whatever. Did Tim from the other night call you?"

Given that Jenna had, unbeknownst to Astrid, given him a fake phone number the answer to that question was easy. Pulling her laptop out of her carry-on, Jenna prayed for wireless Internet so she could check her email while she answered Astrid with as much innocence as she could muster. "No. Did...um, what's his name call you?"

"Jeremy. And no." Astrid let out a big sigh.

"Don't tell me you liked him," Jenna accused.

"Yeah, kinda. Why?"

"Why?" The man hadn't been able to keep his eyes off every female in the bar that night and he was supposed to be Astrid's date, that's why. Jenna couldn't exactly tell her friend that so she threw out her next best piece of ammunition. "For one thing, Jeremy came right out and suggested the four of us go back to his place and have some *fun*."

"So?"

"So, I don't think he was suggesting we play Scrabble. Astrid, Jeremy and Tim were not on that dating website trying to find a meaningful relationship. They were looking for some sort of swinging, group sex, orgy thing." Jenna lowered her voice as she noticed the dark-suited businessman seated across from her seem a bit too interested in the conversation.

"No. I don't think so." Astrid hesitated for a second. "You think?"

"Uh, yeah, I do. Besides that, there is no way the two of them work on Wall Street. I'm sorry, but men who make the kind of money they were pretending to make do not wear cheap polyester jackets. And those shoes." Jenna may not know a lot about a lot of things, but she knew clothes and shoes.

Astrid sighed. "Yeah, you're probably right. Damn. Where are all the good guys hiding? I probably should have waited around for Tex to get off work instead. He may only be a bartender, but at least I knew that upfront."

Jenna hated to encourage Astrid's flirtations with any man further, but going home with Tex would have been a better plan than picking up two guys on the Internet and inviting them out for drinks. Maybe if Astrid were dating Tex, Jenna could at least get some good cowboy dialogue out of listening to him talk.

"Oh well. I better get back to work. The evil witch is roaming about and I don't want her to catch me on the phone on a—*horror*—personal call."

Jenna smiled, thankful—not for the first time—that she didn't have a boss to report to. But if she didn't get this new book written that might not be the case for much longer. Saying goodbye to Astrid, Jenna connected to the airport's wireless Internet and scrolled through the emails that had accumulated since the night before.

Amid the junk, one email stood out. *Romancing the Romance Reviews.* RRR was infamous for being tough. Swallowing hard, Jenna clicked the email open, tapping her foot against the leg of her chair as the browser seemed to take forever to load. Finally, the review was in front of her.

Jenna skimmed the summery of the plot from her last release, heading straight to the end. That was always the most important part to read, the reviewer's opinion, which is when Jenna blurted out a loud "What?" that had the businessman across from her raising an eyebrow.

Jenna read through the review again, and then again, but it didn't change anything. The reviewer found the story "fairly entertaining" and the characters "moderately compelling", but none of that mattered because trumping all the not-so-complimentary compliments was the one devastating line that overshadowed the rest.

Unfortunately, I cannot give Ms. Block a rave review, nor recommend this book to others, because of my disappointment with the sensual scenes, what there were of them, which bored me nearly to tears.

As Jenna sat in stunned silence, contemplating if her agent had read this review and was ready to dump her because her sex scenes were "boring", an announcement cut through the air.

"Attention all passengers on Flight 921 to Tulsa. The flight's departure has been delayed."

Can this trip get any worse? Honestly, what else could possibly go wrong?

A shadow fell across Jenna's laptop, blocking out the light from the overhead fluorescent bulbs. Her gaze traveled up from the brown scuffed shoes, to the gray polyester pinstripe suit held up by a black belt, and ended finally at the horrendously bad toupee.

"Excuse me. Is this seat taken?"

"Um. No." Balancing her laptop on her knees, she managed to stifle her annoyed sigh and move her bag off the seat next to her.

"Thanks." The man displayed yellowed teeth along with his smile. His tattered and overstuffed bag dropped to the floor with a thud. He sat with a grunt and a *whoosh* of vinyl while squinting at the flight information. "Looks like they updated the departure time."

Afraid to look, she did anyway. "A two-hour delay?" Come on.

"That's what they say now. I flew this route last month and after a bunch of delays, it ended up being totally cancelled. Had to spend the night in the airport and fly out the next morning."

Jenna stifled a groan.

She'd had to ask, and now the answer was obvious. Yes, this trip could indeed get worse. Apparently, her hell had only just begun.

$*$

"Holy fuck." Mustang hissed in a breath as the woman lying between his splayed thighs scraped her teeth none too gently one last time up his now spent cock. His body twitched as the pleasure and pain mingled and became nearly, but not quite, unbearable.

"Jeez, you can say that again." Slade laughed next to him with his own half of the pair of eighteen-year-old best friends they'd picked up. They'd found the girls at a bar after stopping in town to rest for the night.

Slade's girl rolled off him to lie on her back, panting from the wild ride Slade had provided. Her silicone-filled tits stood straight up, saluting the ceiling of the trailer.

Mustang glanced down at his portion of the matching set as her mouth finally released him with an audible *pop* and she lounged on her side. Eyeing her torpedo-like boobs as they defied gravity, he wondered if the two friends had gotten a two-for-one deal on their breast implant surgery.

His quarter of their cozy foursome began running her fingernail over him, playfully tracing the line of hair that ran from his stomach straight down to the organ she'd gotten intimately familiar with over the past hour. Practically purring, she asked, "You ready to go again, cowboy?"

Mustang glanced down at Junior, who was curled up in pretty much a fetal position at the moment after the tongue lashing he'd just received. Mustang considered himself in good shape, but damn...

"A man needs a little bit of recovery time. You gotta give me a few minutes, darlin'."

He searched his memory for the brunette's name. He knew one was Candy and one was Destiny. Destiny had dark hair because both words started with a "d". That meant Slade's girl, the blonde, was Candy.

"That's okay. You can watch for now." Destiny's suggestion was accompanied by a smirk.

Mustang watched, not understanding what she meant until she crawled over Slade and settled herself in between Candy's legs, who Mustang noticed for the first time had blond hair on her head and black hair on her bush.

Destiny's hands parted the flesh there and what he knew was a very talented tongue shot out. It thrust into Candy, causing her to jolt and then do some purring of her own. Next to him, Slade's brows shot up to his hairline.

"You know, Slade. I liked your idea about trying to find twins, but there's no way sisters would do *that*." If they did, there's no way he'd want to be around to see it. That would be too freaking weird. Mustang's gaze focused back on the two females on the bed.

After a few speechless moments, during which both he and Slade watched the girl-on-girl action with rapt attention, Mustang sat up. "Well, that's it. I'm ready to go again."

Mustang flipped a leg over Candy, who was lying on her back. He kneeled behind her head, and slid into her mouth while the other girl, butt in the air, continued her work between her friend's thighs.

He watched as the tip of the girl's pink tongue continued flicking out to tease the other girl's clit, now swollen and distended from being worked so hard. Slade stayed motionless

"Come on, Slade. There's plenty of room left for you to slip in somewhere." Mustang grinned down at the porno-worthy scene in front of him, enjoying the view.

Slade shook his head, grinning. "Give me another minute, man. That was quite a workout I just had."

Mustang laughed. "All right. Your loss."

Then Candy started to come, her cries muffled by his girth down her throat. Mustang closed his eyes and groaned, loving the vibrations of the girl's cries.

That must have finally done it for Slade, who in spite of claiming exhaustion had begun to sit up and take notice the moment the two girls went at it. Now he fully rose to the occasion and grabbed a foil packet, about to cover himself.

Tired of being sucked, Mustang craved something different. "Hey, Slade, you wanna switch?"

Slade laughed. "Sure. Whatever."

Mustang grabbed the condom and covered himself. Knee-walking across the bed, he slid with one thrust into Destiny's inviting pussy, high in the air before him.

Not wanting Destiny to feel left out on account of Candy's multiple orgasms, he wet his thumb with saliva and stuck it in her ass while his other hand reached around and found her clit. He pressed his finger deeper into her and she began to shake.

With his eyelids squeezed tightly shut, Mustang let himself just feel. Eyes closed, he could concentrate on all the sensations bombarding him. The scents of sweat and sex that permeated the air. The heat of the body rhythmically squeezing both his cock and finger. The feel of the ass banging back against him as he pounded into her.

At the other end of the chain of linked bodies Slade came. Mustang let himself follow right behind.

Tonight had turned out to be one hell of a good time. Tomorrow they'd be in Tulsa. Who knew what that city would bring? Mustang couldn't wait to find out.

Chapter Four

"Mustang Jackson has drawn one rank bull for the long round. Ballbreaker is out of B&G Stock Contractors and he sure is doing them proud. He's unridden in sixteen times out."

Jenna perched on the edge of the hotel room bed, transcribing every word the television commentators said. Well, most of the words anyway. These guys talked *fast*. Throw in the thick cowboy drawl on the one guy, and her job of capturing their conversation word for word got even more difficult.

But who was she to look a gift horse in the mouth? She knew she'd lucked out when she stumbled upon bull riding on one of the many, *many* sports channels on cable in her surprisingly nice Tulsa hotel room after she checked in for the romance convention.

"You're right, Jim. This bull sure is rank. He's up for Bull of the Year, but if Mustang Jackson can stay on him, he'll ensure his place in the short round and could take tonight's competition."

"What's your prediction, JW? Will Jackson ride this bull tonight and break Ballbreaker's perfect record of buck-offs?"

"Well, Mustang has a habit of getting into his hand a little bit so I don't know."

"One thing we do know is that Mustang Jackson can't afford to make any mistakes here tonight in Kansas City, the last stop before next week's championship in Tulsa."

Jenna frowned. What did they mean next week in Tulsa? The competition was this week. In fact, she had already spoken to the concierge and found out the time and place and how much a cab would cost to take her there tomorrow night.

The men continued to chatter on the screen while Jenna switched to her web browser and did a television listings search. And *dammit*, while she did, they were saying all sorts of good stuff she wanted to write down.

"It seems they're having some trouble getting Mustang settled on Ballbreaker. He's up and off him again, so we'll go on over to Slade Bower, already in the chute on top of Ace in the Hole. Who are you picking in this match up, JW?"

"Slade sometimes has a habit of getting just a little bit leaned back. I don't know enough about this bull to say for sure, but this close to the championship, Slade needs to focus and ride every bull."

"You're right. Mustang Jackson's been chasing Slade Bower in the standings all year and, as you said, every bull counts here tonight with Tulsa just a week away."

Trying to memorize the key phrases like "leaned back" and something about being chased in the standings until she could jot them down, Jenna found the show she was watching listed on the program guide.

"Encore presentation." *Double dammit.* No wonder. The show was a repeat. She switched back over to the document on her computer screen and began to type frantically again, pissed she'd missed good dialogue, just as the phone rang.

"Shit!"

Writing this stupid cowboy book was going to kill her...or at least give her an ulcer. Jenna reached for the room's phone on the nightstand and almost dumped her laptop on the floor in the process.

"Hello?" She fumbled with the receiver on her shoulder and tried to listen, type and talk all at once.

"Hey, Jenna. It's Barb." The chipper voice of one of her closest author friends came through the phone line. "I'm in the bar with a few of the other girls and we're about to head into the Wild West Welcome Dinner. Are you coming down?"

Jenna sighed, torn between starvation and television rodeo research. Hunger eventually won out. Besides, she'd more than likely get all she needed tomorrow night at the rodeo. She hoped.

"Yeah, I'm coming. I'll meet you in the ballroom, I guess."

"Are you getting dressed up? It's cowboy-themed attire, remember."

God help her, why did every meal at these conventions require some sort of ridiculous costume on the part of the authors? Jenna spied the boots she'd thrown in her suitcase to wear to the rodeo, figuring she'd look inappropriate in high heels amid the cowgirls and cow dung. After checking in and unpacking, she had already changed into jeans from her traveling sweat suit. Those, combined with the boots, would just have to do.

"Um, yeah. I'm dressed." Put like that, Jenna didn't consider it a lie at all.

"Okay. Good. We'll save you a seat at the table. You can't miss me. I'll be the one in the pink cowboy hat with a blond Dolly Parton wig."

Jenna giggled at that image. "Thanks, Barb. See you in a minute."

She reluctantly clicked off the television set just as the cowboy, Slade What's-His-Name, hit the dirt.

Slade... Good name. Jenna would have to write that down to use in her book.

Chapter Five

Evaluating that night's possibilities, Mustang's gaze swept the females in the stands until it landed on one woman who made him stop dead in his perusal.

He jumped up onto the rail of the chute and hissed to Slade, "Second section, fourth row back, reddish-brown hair pulled back in a ponytail, black turtleneck."

In the process of tugging the rope that stretched beneath the bull and winding it once around his gloved hand, Slade frowned up at Mustang from the animal's back. "I'm in the middle of taking my wrap and you're pointing out some woman to me? In a turtleneck, no less? Since when are you interested in women whose tits aren't hanging out?"

"This woman's different, Slade. I can tell." The bull hopped once in the chute and Mustang quickly reached over and grabbed the back of Slade's vest, steadying him on the animal's back.

"Dammit, Mustang, quit distracting me." Slade settled himself again and then gave a nod. The cowboy on the ground swung the gate open to release both bull and rider into the arena.

"Talk to you more when you get off," Mustang called after him.

As Mustang watched his friend disappear into a cloud of dust, Chase Reese hopped up onto the rail next to him.

"Slade's amazing. It's like he's glued onto that bull. I wish I could do that. I went two for ten last series." The kid had been favored for Rookie of the Year until he'd hit a dry streak.

"That's because you look at the ground." Mustang followed Slade's progress while the bull spun around to the left without deviation, from one end of the arena to the other.

The eight-second buzzer sounded and Slade released the rope wrapped around his hand. He jumped off the bull, hit the ground with his shoulder and then rolled to avoid a hoof to the ribcage before the bullfighters redirected the charging animal away from him.

"I do what?"

Seeing his friend was safe, Mustang took the time to answer Chase's question. Damn, had he ever been this young? The kid probably didn't even have to shave once a week.

"You're looking down at the ground while you ride. If you look there, you're gonna end up there. It's a fact. Now, 'scuse me. I gotta talk to Slade."

Leaving the kid with an amazed expression on his face, as if he'd just been handed all the secrets of the universe, Mustang jumped down to go meet Slade behind the chutes.

"Hey, man. Good ride. That bull was one hell of a spinner, huh?"

Slade laughed and pulled the tape from around his wrist where it held the glove on his riding hand firmly in place. "Hell yeah. They weren't kidding when they said he came out of the spinner pen. Felt like I was on a ride at the county fair."

"Now we're both done riding for the night, we have to formulate a plan," Mustang began.

"For what?"

"To reel in that woman I told you about."

Slade dismissed that with a wave of his hand. "Just do whatever it is you usually do."

Mustang shook his head. "The usual bullshit isn't going to work on her."

Slade sighed. "Where did you say she's sitting?"

Ha! Slade had given in and was actually showing some interest. Smiling, Mustang narrowed his eyes and easily found her again in the stands. She was writing feverishly while trying to watch the rider in the arena at the same time. He tilted his head toward the section directly behind them. "Far end of the fourth row."

"What the hell is she doing?" Slade frowned as he watched her.

"Hell if I know, but I think she's taking notes. See what I mean? This woman is special. She isn't going to just fall into our bed."

Her hair wasn't huge, she wasn't made up like a showgirl and her clothes showed curves but not an inch of skin. She was different, which was what had drawn Mustang's attention to her in the first place.

Since Slade had been in his strange funk lately, Mustang figured he'd try something unusual. Hell, even the two eighteen-year-olds going at each other in front of them barely got a rise out of his friend. Mustang was running out of ideas, but this woman... She was pretty much the opposite of their usual conquest and that might be exactly what they needed. It was worth a shot to cheer Slade up. Besides, never opposed to trying new things, he could use a bit of a change himself once in a while.

"Mustang, she's probably a damned reporter. That's all I need, to be featured in some exposé. I can see the headline now. 'Slade Bower, third-ranking bull rider in the world, propositions reporter for a threesome with former Rookie of the Year, Mustang Jackson.' That will go over real well with the fans in the Bible Belt." Slade scowled at Mustang. "Pick someone else. How about the one bouncing up and down over there? She's about to pop right out of that top. You might want to keep an eye on her."

Mustang glanced her way. "Yeah, I saw her already. I'm set on the other one."

Laughing, Slade shook his head. "Good luck 'cause I can just about see the stick up her ass from here. That one is wound tight, but you go for it, man, and I'll enjoy watching you get shot down."

Mustang raised a brow. "Is that a challenge, my friend?"

Slade let out a short laugh. "No, it's the truth."

"Well, I think you're wrong. Sometimes it's the quiet ones that are the wildest once you get them naked."

"And you think you can get her naked?"

Mustang nodded. "Yup. I do."

"Well, I'd like to see that."

Grinning, Mustang slapped his friend on the back. "Don't worry. You'll be there too."

Slade shook his head. "*Maybe*, and that is a big maybe, you might be able to get that woman naked, with enough alcohol and bullshit, but no frigging way will she agree to both of us. Never in a million years."

Feeling cocky and never one to resist a challenge, Mustang crossed his arms and dug in his heels. "We'll see. You willing to make a bet on that?"

Mirroring Mustang, Slade crossed his own arms over his chest. "Yes, we will see and, yes, I am. What do you want to bet?"

Mustang grinned. Slade was showing more interest in their extracurricular activities than he had in weeks. Maybe he had really just been bored like he said. Perhaps what they both needed was a good challenge. Mustang knew to his core this woman would provide at least that, but more than likely, so much more. Besides, he really enjoyed a good bet.

"How about the loser has to buy the winner a new pair of chaps?"

Slade grinned. "I could use me a new pair of chaps, so you're on."

Glancing back at the stands to search again for the object of their wager, Mustang frowned.

"Where the hell is she? Slade, she's gone." He spun back and found the last person he ever expected to see standing right there next to Slade.

"Excuse me. I was wondering if I could ask you two a few questions."

His angel in black spoke with the sexiest voice he'd ever heard. From the sound of her, she was from back east and definitely not a local, just like he'd thought. Mustang only hoped Slade's theory about her being a reporter was wrong.

He saw Slade raise an eyebrow and cockily turn to him, waiting expectantly for Mustang to answer her question—what had that been again? Oh, yeah, she wanted to ask them questions. Interesting.

Suddenly face-to-face with her, Mustang stumbled over his usually smooth tongue a bit. "Um...yeah...sure, darlin'. What do you need?"

She extended her hand and broke out into a smile. "Great. Let me introduce myself first. I'm Jenna Block."

Not remembering the last time a woman had stopped to shake his hand before they fucked, Mustang smiled. He took hold of her hand, noticing how her hazel eyes had tinges of both gold and green in them.

She had a good, strong grip too. He liked that in a woman. "Pleasure to meet you. I'm Mustang Jackson."

Mustang took a second to admire the rest of Jenna, from the tip of her brunette ponytail to the tops of her shiny black, pointy-toed cowboy boots—and if those boots of hers had walked anywhere besides the concrete sidewalks of a city street before tonight, Mustang would eat his hat.

After the quick visual sweep, he continued the introductions. "This here's Slade Bower."

He turned to introduce Slade, only to find the man was in the midst of his own full-body sweep of Ms. Jenna Block.

Oh yeah, now which one of them wanted to get her drunk and into bed naked?

Jenna turned and shook Slade's hand as he mumbled a greeting and barely wrenched his gaze up from the outline of her sweater-covered tits in time before she caught him with his eyes where they shouldn't have been.

Mustang grinned. Yup, Slade didn't seem bored anymore.

"Wow." She released a breathy laugh, shaking her head and glancing from one to another.

Mustang raised a brow at that. "Wow what?"

She blushed prettily. "Sorry, I'm being silly. It's just that I recognize your names from television. It's quite the coincidence I saw you on TV yesterday and now I'm talking to you in person."

"You watch bull riding on television?" At least that surprising statement had knocked some coherent words out of Slade.

"Mmm hmm. Well, I mean not *usually* but I have recently. It's a long story. Look, would you be willing to let me buy you both a drink so we can sit down while we talk and I ask you a few questions?"

The shock on Slade's face at *her* proposing they get a drink together nearly made Mustang laugh out loud. Oh yeah, those new chaps were as good as his, and it was Slade's wallet that would be a little lighter after the purchase.

Mustang controlled his glee and answered for both of them, forcing himself to sound casual. "I guess we could sit down with you...for a few minutes, anyway." *Before we go back to the trailer and I show Slade that there is no stick up your ass, though there easily could be some Mustang in there if you'd like...*

Oh, he was a dirty boy. Maybe Ms. Jenna Block should spank him. Mustang had never tried that. Could be interesting. He'd keep it in mind for later.

Mustang enjoyed that vision as the woman in his newest fantasy flashed him her perfect smile again. "Great. Is there somewhere within walking distance we can go? I came in a cab."

"Well, there's our trailer. It's close and the drinks there are free." Mustang grinned, waiting for her reaction while knowing there was no way she'd fall prey to them that easily. What would be the fun if there wasn't even a little bit of a challenge?

She didn't prove him wrong as she raised one brow cockily. "Is there someplace *public* we can go?"

Mustang smiled at her sidestepping the invitation as Slade jumped in and answered her. "There's a nice public bar across the street. We can walk there."

"Wonderful." She looked around at the rapidly emptying stands. "Is this thing over for the night or is this an intermission?"

"No, we're done for tonight. We just have to stash our gear." *And shower in case we do all end up naked.* Mustang had never wanted to get a woman naked this badly. "Can you give us ten minutes then we'll meet you right over there by the exit?"

She nodded. "Sure."

As she waited safely behind them by the entrance, the two headed out of the public part of the arena. Along the way, they grabbed their ropes from where they'd looped them over the railing.

"Okay, admit it. You like her," Mustang accused Slade once they were out of hearing range.

Slade scowled at him as they walked. "Doesn't matter either way. We're not taking her back to the trailer because I'm telling you I'm convinced now more than ever that she's some kind of reporter from back east. She shook your hand, for God's sake."

Mustang considered that as well as her odd choice of the turtleneck when the rest of the females in the crowd had worn T-shirts or boob-baring low-cut numbers. Her dark blue jeans had an actual crease down the leg as if she'd ironed them. Then there were those shiny black boots that city folk wore for fashion not utility, the huge black leather satchel slung on her one shoulder that most likely carried the notebook he'd seen her writing in before, the way she carried herself, with confidence and polish...

The fact she seemed to know their names but knew nothing else about bull riding confused Mustang the most. If she was a true fan or a sports reporter she would have known that with Slade ranked third, barring any re-rides, the second and first-place riders that had followed him were the final two rides for the night and the competition would continue tomorrow.

Mustang shook his head. "She's something, I'll give you that much, but I don't think it's a reporter."

"We'll see." Slade shoved his vest and rope into his gear bag.

"Yes, we will." And in just a few minutes too. This could be the most fun he and Slade had had in a long time, and Mustang couldn't wait.

Chapter Six

"I don't even know where to start." The sophisticated, pretty brunette sighed and stared down at the yellow legal pad covered in chicken scratch. Slade assumed they were the notes she had scribbled during the competition.

"I find it's best to start with beer and move on to the hard stuff later." Mustang grinned, his entire body turned toward her as the three sat at a small, slightly sticky table in the rapidly filling bar across the street from the arena.

She laughed at Mustang's lame joke. Slade shook his head, amazed as always at how Mustang could charm females of any age including, apparently, city-slicker reporters.

Leaned way back in his chair, Slade ignored the interested looks they, as an unlikely trio, were getting from the other bull riders slowly filtering into the bar. Instead, he watched the mystery woman smile playfully at Mustang.

"I meant I don't know where to start with my questions, but yeah, let's order a pitcher, if that's all right with you two?" She glanced from Mustang to Slade.

"You drink beer?" Slade raised a brow at her.

"Yes. Why?" She challenged him with a raised brow of her own.

Slade didn't hide how he let his gaze roam over her. "By the look of you, it seems to me that you'd be more the Chardonnay type."

She pursed her lips at the veiled insult. "Actually, when I do drink wine, I prefer a nice Merlot."

Beneath the light of the neon beer sign, Mustang signaled the waitress for a pitcher before he turned to stare at Slade. "In all the years I've known you, I don't think I've ever once heard you say the word Chardonnay."

Slade scowled at his friend. "Hey, I know stuff. Just 'cause I don't choose to share it with you—what the devil are you writing?"

Slade turned back to the damn woman, who had flipped to a clean page in her pad and was scribbling furiously as he and Mustang bickered.

She paused and looked up at him. "Um, I'm taking notes."

"Of our conversation?" Slade sputtered.

Pen poised above the page, she nodded. "Yeah. This is great dialogue."

Slade's mouth twisted in a scowl. "It's not *dialogue*. It's two friends talking over drinks after a ride." And he wasn't so sure he wanted her writing it all down.

"Well, it will be dialogue once I write it."

Slade leaned forward in his chair, across the table and closer to the woman and her infernal notes. "About that. Before we go any further with this, I think we need to know exactly who you are and what you are doing here."

"I'm Jenna Block and I'm a writer—"

"A writer." Slade shot Mustang an I-told-you-so look.

She nodded. "Yes. I write romance novels."

With a huge grin, Mustang returned Slade's I-told-you-so look times two before turning back to her. "Romance novels. Really? Now, *that* sounds interesting."

Jenna Block, romance writer, shrugged. "It can be, but the research on this one is killing me. I'm writing about a cowboy and I decided to have him ride bulls in the rodeo."

"Well, that explains the notes." Mustang looked pointedly at Slade. "My suspicious friend here thought for a minute you might be a reporter writing an exposé about the two hottest bull riders on the circuit."

She giggled. "If I were, then I'd probably know what the hell I was writing about. As it is, I'm totally lost and I'm afraid if I'm not accurate with the facts I'll get killed by the reviewers."

Mustang's patented chick-magnet grin appeared again. "Well then, it's a good thing you found us, because you won't find two more knowledgeable cowboys anywhere when it comes to bulls."

Or bullshit. Unnoticed by Jenna, who beyond all reason seemed completely enthralled by Mustang's charm, Slade shook his head.

Jenna. At least the woman didn't have a name that ended in a "y" or an "i" and sounded like it belonged to a stripper. Slade might even have a chance of remembering it for the rest of the night. At least he remembered it now while he was here talking with her. That was more than he could say for the last half dozen or so girls he'd had sex with.

Slade's train of thought regarding female names was interrupted when Jenna surprised them both by asking, totally out of the blue, "What ever happened with Ballbreaker?"

Mustang nearly choked at Jenna's question. "Excuse me?"

"You were having trouble getting on Ballbreaker in Kansas City. The announcers said he was—" Jenna shuffled to a different page and read, "—'unridden after sixteen times out'. Whatever happened? Did you ride him?"

Slade enjoyed being able to give her the answer on Mustang's behalf for that question. "Nope. Mustang hit the dirt in two seconds. Ballbreaker's still unridden after seventeen outs."

"Hey! He was all bunched up in the back of the chute. I never did get myself seated on him right."

"Yeah, yeah. Whatever." Slade grinned.

Mustang scowled.

Meanwhile, Jenna scribbled furiously and then looked up at them both. "Thank you so much for agreeing to help me. I mean I hear the announcers talking about 'the draw' and then 'the draft' and I don't know the difference. Then there's the 'short round' and the 'long round' and 'into his hand' and 'away from his hand'." She hesitated. "And I have other more...personal questions too."

Intrigued, Slade couldn't stop himself from asking, "Like what kind of personal questions?"

Beneath the blue neon, as the waitress slapped down the pitcher and three plastic cups, Slade could have sworn Jenna blushed at his question.

"Like, um, I see some guys wear helmets and some don't, and you all seem to wear those thick, stiff, protective vests, but do you also wear, um, cups?" She whispered the last word.

Across the table, Mustang choked on the beer he'd poured and taken a gulp out of just as Jenna asked that question. You'd think the man would know enough not to drink while this surprising woman was talking.

Slade grinned at how embarrassed she'd become. Knowing exactly what she meant, he played dumb anyway. "Cups? What d'ya mean?"

Red-faced and looking ready to crawl under the tiny cocktail table, Jenna mumbled, "You know, like a jock strap?"

Mustang, finally recovering from his coughing and sputtering, shook his head. "No, ma'am. We don't wear cups."

Taking a gulp of his own beer, Slade enjoyed seeing Jenna's eyes open wide at Mustang's answer. "You don't? But there's a lot of...bouncing and... I mean, it looks really dangerous. What if you get stepped on, you know, down there?"

"First of all, no little plastic cup is going to help if a two-thousand-pound bull steps on you. Besides, I've been riding for six years and been stepped on plenty of times in many places and all my parts are still in perfect working order. Wanna see?" Mustang reached to release the well-worn Rookie of the Year belt buckle at his waist, teasing her.

"That's okay. Maybe later." She cocked a brow, bouncing back from her temporary bout of shyness to shoot Mustang down, which Slade enjoyed a bit too much.

Abandoning his belt, Mustang raised his plastic cup to her in salute. "Okay, later then. It's a date. Oh, and in case you're wondering, Slade here's parts all work too. Most of the time, anyway."

Slade frowned and narrowed his eyes at his supposed friend over that remark.

Avoiding eye contact with Slade, which he was kind of grateful for at the moment, Jenna nodded to Mustang. "Good to know. Thanks."

Was she blushing again?

"You're such an idiot," Slade mumbled, before noticing she was back to writing. He pointed at her. "See, Mustang. Now she's gonna write all that shit down."

Jenna directed her attention back to Mustang. "About that. Your name, *Mustang*, how'd you get it?"

Jumping at the chance for revenge, Slade dove right in. "That's simple. It's because he's hung like a horse."

"Yeah, right. Very funny." Jenna scowled at Slade and then turned to Mustang. "Come on. Really. How did you get the nickname? Do you own a Ford Mustang or something?"

"Nope." Mustang grinned wide.

"Your first horse was a mustang?"

Still grinning broadly, he shook his head at her once again. "Nope."

"You are really named for the size of your..." Her eyes dropped to Mustang's crotch before she yanked them back up.

Slade laughed at her. "Well, it's not like his mama took one look at him naked in the hospital and named him that when he was born. His given name is Michael Jackson, but would you want to be a cowboy with the same name as some 1980s pop singer?"

"*Slade.* Jeez. Thanks a lot." Mustang scowled at him over the rim of his beer cup.

"What? I'm allowed to tell her about the size of your dick but not that your real name is Michael Jackson?"

Mustang scowled. "That's right."

Slade rolled his eyes and turned back to Jenna, who appeared to still be having trouble finding a safe place to look when he made eye contact with her. "Anyway, when Mustang here started riding he tried to go by Mike Jackson, but we found out everyone in his high school used to call him Mustang because one of the girls he had nailed commented on how big he was. The name stuck."

Slade noted Jenna's cheeks flush again as she listened to him before she recovered her composure. "Okay. Thanks."

Mustang, apparently over the anger that Slade had outed him about his real name, leaned toward Jenna. "I'd be happy to show you if you'd like. For your research."

"Thanks. I'll keep that in mind." Still pink-cheeked, Jenna stared hard at her pad, flipping through the pages of scrawl again.

Slade sipped his beer and waited for her to find whatever she was looking for while he enjoyed watching her flustered.

"My head is spinning. I don't have much time here in Tulsa, but there's so much great stuff you two can give me."

Mustang shook his head and laughed. "Oh, darlin'. You have no idea."

She shot him an indulgent look. "I meant for the book."

"Sure, for that too." Mustang grinned charmingly, sliding her untouched beer cup toward her not so subtly.

"What do you have so far for this book of yours? Maybe we should start by taking a look at it," Slade offered, anxious to get the conversation off Mustang's dick.

Jenna seemed surprised at his suggestion. Hell, he was shocked as shit himself that he was actually interested, in both the woman and her book.

Slade realized this was probably the most conversation he'd exchanged with a female in years. Usually they skipped the talking part and went right from drinking to fucking, sometimes skipping the drinking portion altogether, depending on how willing she was.

Jenna reached into her bag. "I printed out what I've written so far. I know it's a lot to ask, but could you take a look at it—just the bull-riding stuff, and maybe some of the cowboy-type stuff—and let me know if it's accurate?"

Slade eyed the thick stack of printed pages, regretting he'd asked, as Mustang said, "Sure, we'll read it. Let's all three of us go on back to our trailer. The light's better there and then we can all get comfortable while we read."

She pursed her lips and shook her head in an excellent imitation of a schoolmarm. "I don't think so. Besides, I don't expect you to read it all right this minute. I can leave that with you and come back tomorrow night. Maybe we can talk again after the show is over?"

The show. Slade smothered a snort at that. "It's not a show. In fact, it's not a rodeo either. You keep saying that, but there's a difference. This here is a professional bull-riders' competition. More importantly, it's the championship."

"Bull-riding competition championship. Okay. Got it." She nodded, writing it all down.

Slade sighed at her constant note-taking. The woman like a damn sponge.

Meanwhile, Mustang leaned back so the beer sign illuminated the printing on the ream of paper she'd laid on the table, and started flipping through it. Suddenly, he burst out laughing. "Buck Wild? You seriously named your bull rider Buck Wild?"

She narrowed her eyes at Mustang. "Yes. So? It's a romance novel. It's supposed to be fun. Besides, a man named Mustang probably shouldn't be picking on my bull rider's name."

Mustang laughed. "All right, I'll concede that point, but you can't fight me on this one. The bull's not in an enclosure. It's a chute. Or a bucking chute. Nobody, 'cept maybe city folk, call it an enclosure."

Scribbling furiously, she wrote that down. "Good. Thank you. See? This is exactly the kind of stuff I need from you. That's perfect. Can you make comments in the margins when you find mistakes like that?"

Not remembering the last time he'd written anything besides signing paychecks at the bank or autographs in the stands, Slade had to think if they even had a pen or pencil in the trailer. He didn't think so. They had better swipe one from the bar.

While Slade pondered their lack of writing instruments, he noticed Mustang had gotten rather quiet, engrossed in the pages. Suddenly, Mustang's eyebrows shot up into his hairline.

"You're skipping right to the sex scenes, aren't you?" Jenna accused, obviously noticing Mustang's reaction too.

Sex scenes? Slade's ears perked up at that. Hmm. Maybe he wasn't sorry they'd offered to read this thing.

Jenna reached to snatch the papers back, but Mustang was faster and whipped them over his head and out of her reach. "No you don't, darlin'. This here is the interesting part. Not realistic, but interesting all the same."

Her eyes flew open wide. "What do you mean *not* realistic?"

Slade wondered the same thing, dying to get his hands on those pages.

Mustang referred to the papers again. "Come on. Women don't come that fast or that easy. Trust me, I know. He barely touches her in this and she's all 'ooh, ahh, I'm coming'. Give me a break."

Coming? What the hell kind of books did this woman write? Slade had to clench his fist to stop himself from grabbing the papers from Mustang.

Jenna, the apparently naughty author, scowled. "Romance is supposed to be fantasy."

Mustang snorted. "Oh, it's fantasy all right. And the guy parts..." He shook his head, laughing.

Jenna crossed her arms. "What, exactly, is wrong with the guy parts?"

Mustang waved the pages at her. "Men don't think like this and men definitely don't act or talk like this, especially in the middle of fucking... Uh, I mean *making love* as you put it."

Slade was seconds away from snatching those pages away from Mustang to see what the hell he was talking about.

"Oh really. So tell me, Mustang, since you're so smart when it comes to men and women, what would you do differently?"

Mustang leaned forward in his chair, abandoning the pages on the table, but Slade was too intrigued in the live action now to worry much about the written stuff.

His face close to Jenna's, Mustang kept his voice so low Slade had to lean in to hear what he said to her. "You want to know what turns a woman on, Miss Block? What's the quickest way for a man to get her hot and wet in the panties?"

Jenna's expression became neutral, but not before Slade noticed her look the tiniest bit shocked at the panty comment.

"Do tell, since you're such an expert."

"It's this." Mustang reached out and lightly tapped her forehead. "A woman's erogenous zone is right there, in her head. You write about touching this or kissing that, but foreplay starts in a woman's brain. If a man can get in there, then all the rest is just a formality. Write about that, what's inside, and don't worry so much about who's putting what where."

Mustang let his finger trail slowly down the side of her face and across her lips before he broke contact and sat back in his chair again. Slade saw Jenna lean in and follow Mustang, like a compass arrow drawn to true north, before she cleared her throat and straightened up in her chair.

The man was a master at reeling them in, and for the first time since they'd been hanging out together, Slade felt a little bit jealous. Even though he knew he'd always be invited in on the action, this time, with this woman, Slade wished he'd been the one manning the fishing line instead of Mustang.

Slade watched Jenna's throat work as she swallowed. "It's late. I better call a cab."

Mustang captured and held her gaze. "It's not that late, darlin'."

Jenna shook her head. "I have a conference back at the hotel that starts at nine in the morning."

Mustang leaned in close again. "Slade and I can drive you back to your hotel in plenty of time for your conference in the morning. I promise."

She shook her head again. "I can't."

Mustang's face lit with a grin. "But you want to."

It sounded more like a statement of fact than a question to Slade. It sure as hell looked like Jenna wanted to.

She swallowed hard and, without admitting anything, repeated, "I can't."

Mustang's hand covered hers. "Give me one reason why not?"

Somehow the discussion had gone from book research to the subject of the three of them getting into bed in a blink of an eye. Slade hadn't even noticed it happening, but something had. Somehow Jenna and Mustang were now negotiating sex. What the hell?

Jenna took a deep breath. "I'm not going to spend the night with the two of you because I'm not one of your bimbo rodeo— excuse me—*bull-riding* groupies."

"The groupies generally don't ride the bulls, and they're known as buckle bunnies. Might want to write that down for the book." Mustang tapped the table near her pad while grinning at his own lame joke, before becoming serious again. "I knew you weren't a bimbo the moment I saw you in the stands in your little black sweater, taking notes during a bull ride."

"You noticed me?"

"Oh, yeah. Slade nearly got bucked off in the chute because I was trying to point you out to him while he was taking his wrap."

Telling the truth to get a girl into bed, that was a new strategy for Mustang, and to Slade's amazement it appeared to be working.

Jenna looked to Slade and he had to laugh as he confirmed the accuracy of Mustang's statement. "It's true."

While she was digesting that, Mustang stood. "Get your stuff together, darlin'. Slade will take care of the bill. After we settle up here we'll drive you back to your hotel."

"No. I said I'd pay. And I can take a cab." Jenna reached into her huge bag, searching for something, most likely her wallet.

"No. Ladies don't pay. Besides, Slade's ranked third in the world. He can afford to buy us one five-dollar pitcher of beer. And there's no way I'm putting you in a cab alone this late when Slade has a perfectly good car sitting next door in the lot. He never gets to drive it because it's always being towed behind my trailer when we travel together."

Jenna glanced at Slade, then went back to studying Mustang for a bit before she finally nodded. "Okay, I'd appreciate a ride to the hotel. Thank you."

Mustang grinned at Slade. "Come on. I'll come up to the bar with you so you can pay the check."

"Yeah, thanks," Slade mumbled. Not that he cared about paying for the pitcher. What bothered him was that Mustang had not only made progress, which for some reason made Slade jealous, but now Mustang was suddenly giving in and giving up on closing the deal when he'd seemed so close. Mustang never gave in until he'd gotten the girl, but tonight that was exactly what he seemed to be doing.

When they'd reached the bar, Slade spun to Mustang. "What the hell were you thinking over there? I've never seen you give up on a woman that easily. How come you're not ordering her some fruity drink and getting her drunk and then taking her back to the trailer?"

"Because this one's special. It's going to take a different lure to reel her in."

Yeah, she was special and different, and that's exactly why Slade didn't want to risk letting her get away. "Do you really think we've got a snowball's chance in hell of ever seeing her again if you let her go now?"

"It's our only chance. I'm telling you, she's not coming back to the trailer tonight and if we push too hard, I guarantee you we'll never see her again. She'll be all scared and hide from us until she leaves Tulsa." Mustang hooked the heel of one boot on the brass bar rail and leaned in, lowering his voice. "She's interested now. We wait until tomorrow, let the idea settle in, and she's all ours, for as long as she's here in town."

Slade considered that, remembering with envy the expression on Jenna's face when Mustang had touched her. "Yeah, maybe. But she's not interested in both of us."

Mustang grinned. "Oh, yeah she is. In both of us."

"You're doing all the talking and she's barely even looked at me."

"That's the thing. She's avoiding looking at you too hard and every time she does, she blushes. Haven't you noticed? You make her nervous." Mustang laughed at that.

Nervous. Great. "That's a good thing?"

"With women it is. And may I say I haven't seen you this interested in a woman in months, maybe a year even."

"I'm not…" Mustang raised a brow skeptically and Slade stopped, mid-denial. "All right. I'm interested. I'll admit it."

The one time Slade actually cared if they got the girl or not, they were willingly driving her home before anything happened. "You sure about taking her back to the hotel now?"

Mustang nodded. "Yup. Positive."

"You think she might invite us up to her room?" Hope sprung eternal inside a horny cowboy.

"If she does, we say no," Mustang ordered.

"Say no? What? Are you crazy? Why?"

"Look. We have her book." Mustang held up the handful of pages he'd grabbed off the table. "She needs us before she can finish this. More importantly, *she knows* she damn well can't do it without us. She's not going anywhere. Believe me, tomorrow night she'll be there in the arena again begging us to give her some more of our valuable time."

"So now we're playing hard to get?"

"Yup." Mustang grinned.

"This plan of yours better work." Slade adjusted his jeans slightly, realizing he'd started to get hard just thinking about Jenna begging them for anything.

Mustang slapped him on the back. "It's good to have you back in action, my friend."

Slade rolled his eyes. "Yeah, yeah. Just don't fuck this one up. Okay?"

"I won't. Don't you worry. I want her as much as you do." Mustang let out a long, low whistle and glanced back at their table. "Damn, she's hot, and those new chaps you're gonna buy me will be a nice bonus too."

Slade followed his friend's gaze to where Jenna sat alone, waiting for them and taking in the crowd with what he suspected was her usual curiosity. They both stood there like idiots staring at the woman neither of them would have that night until Mustang finally blew out a loud breath.

"Damn. Let's go before I change my mind and order that fruity drink. And I'm gonna need the bathroom first when we get back." Mustang adjusted himself within his jeans, shaking his head. "It's been a long time since I've willingly rubbed one out on my own after a competition."

Slade's thoughts exactly, yet he couldn't say he was disappointed he'd be right-handing it tonight instead of going at some nameless, brainless girl. Once you'd set your sights on a prize-winning thoroughbred, just any filly wouldn't do.

Slade pushed a five and two singles toward the waitress to cover the pitcher and her tip. "I'll get the car. You keep those two rookies who are eyeing Jenna off her, and don't do anything stupid to scare her away before I get back."

Mustang grinned so wide, Slade had to stop mid-step toward the door. "What are you grinning at?"

"You know her name."

Yeah, Slade had noticed that himself but was trying not to think too much about it. He shook his head and didn't comment. "I'll meet you outside with the car."

Chapter Seven

"Happy birthday!" Astrid's bright, cheery voice came through the cell phone loud and clear.

"Thanks, Astrid." Jenna stifled a groan. Between the day's full conference agenda and those two tempting cowboys, she couldn't seem to get out of her mind, she'd managed to forget about her thirty-fifth birthday. Until now.

"What are you going to do to celebrate? Ooo, and before I forget, did you go to the rodeo yet?"

Jenna laughed. "The answer to those two questions are one and the same. I was there last night, and I'm just getting ready now to go back tonight, but it isn't a rodeo. It's a bull-riding competition."

"What's the difference?"

"I'm not exactly sure, but it seems to mean quite a bit to the two hot bull riders I had drinks with last night. The same two I'm meeting tonight to discuss my book research."

"You're meeting two hot cowboys for drinks?"

"To discuss my book," Jenna reminded Astrid. She'd spent all last night and half the day trying to convince herself of that as her mind kept wandering back to the two.

"I'm so jealous. I knew I should have come with you." She could almost hear Astrid's pouting through the phone.

"I told you that you could come with me. I have a room all to myself." With a big king-sized bed that would probably accommodate Jenna plus two cowboys. She averted her gaze from the expansive mattress and shook that vision from her mind.

"You know I couldn't take a week off work. But darn it, it would have been perfect. One hot cowboy for you and one for me. Damn, damn, damn! Now I'm pissy. When do you leave for the rodeo?"

Knowing it would be no use, Jenna didn't bother correcting Astrid about the rodeo bull-riding terminology again. "Now. I just called the cab so I'm about to head into the elevator in a minute and wait downstairs in the lobby."

She heard Astrid emit an annoyed sigh. "I want a phone call first thing tomorrow telling me everything. Promise, okay?"

"I promise." Jenna hung up and considered the conversation for a moment.

If Astrid had been there, which man would Jenna have been willing to give her? The funny and cute sandy-haired Mustang with that larger-than-life personality, those big, dreamy blue eyes and the supposedly even bigger... She felt her face heat just thinking about how he'd gotten to her by using just one finger and a few words. Her heart skipped a beat at the thought of what else that one finger could do to her, not to mention the supposedly super-sized rest of him.

Then there was Slade, so sexy, dark and mysterious, hiding behind a wall by letting his friend do most of the talking, all while keeping himself at an emotional arm's length. He made her want to peel back his many layers, as well as his clothes. She was sure what lay underneath—in both cases—would be well worth the trouble. It would be if the way he made her blush and sent a flutter straight to her core whenever she looked at him was any indication.

Jenna easily pictured breaking down Slade's walls and him finally letting himself go as they tumbled into bed together. But she could also imagine Mustang braced above her while staring into her eyes as she got lost in his ever-present smile.

It would be an impossible choice, but judging by the way Mustang kept inviting her back to *their* trailer so the three of them could *all* get comfortable, she obviously wouldn't need to make a choice if she didn't want to. As she had lain in bed the night before, hot and bothered and picturing the two cowboys, there had been many scenarios running through her head where she didn't. Her sleep had been crappy, but her fantasies had been pretty damned good.

Normal, average, borderline-boring suburban women didn't have a *ménage a trois* with cowboys they barely knew and would never see again. Did they? On the other hand, she was thirty-five and single, and very capable of making her own decisions.

Swallowing hard, Jenna tried to ignore, not for the first time today, the dampness soaking her panties. She glanced at her flushed reflection in the room's full-length mirror, second guessing leaving her hair down for the evening, or more accurately, why she'd left it loose. She'd wanted to look sexy for the two cowboys who were only supposed to help her with the bull-riding facts. Little had she known they'd be inspiring her sexual fantasies instead.

Jenna studied her reflection harder. She'd chosen a black knee-length knit dress that looked surprisingly good when she'd tried it on with bare legs and her black cowboy boots.

What if she did have sex with them both? Who would it hurt? As Jenna grabbed her bag with her notes and wallet she knew the answer to that question. She could get hurt. But damn, her body, which had already started to get excited at the thought of seeing the two again, didn't seem to care about that.

✳

At the arena, Jenna stepped up to the window, wallet in hand. There wasn't much of a line because apparently everyone else had purchased their tickets in advance and gone straight in.

"One ticket please." Jenna slid her credit card across the counter.

The young woman behind the glass took it and looked at her card closely. "Your name is Jenna Block?"

Taken aback, Jenna nodded. "Yes, it is."

The girl slid an envelope along with the credit card beneath the partition. "This ticket was left for you."

Confused, Jenna didn't question it, but took the envelope, shoving her credit card back into her wallet. "Um. Okay. Thanks."

Things got even stranger when she showed the ticket to the guy at the door. If his amused look that took her in from head to toe didn't alert her something was off, the fact the man directed her right up to the front row of seats directly behind the bucking chutes did.

She sat and looked around. From there, she would be able to count the hairs on the bulls' backs.

"Hey, you made it."

Jenna narrowed her eyes at Mustang as he swung up onto the railing to be eyelevel with her. "You left me that ticket, didn't you?"

"I sure did. Great seats, huh?"

"Yeah, but I'm thinking this is the special bimbo bull-rider-groupie section."

"Shh." He leaned in closer. "Keep your voice down. The woman sitting two seats over is the wife of the number one rider in the world. But actually, I think she's Brazilian and can't speak English so I guess she didn't understand you anyway."

Jenna crossed her arms. "And tube-top girl next to her?"

Mustang grinned. "All right, she may be a bit of a bimbo, but she's the girlfriend of one of the rookies. He's young and doesn't know any better. He'll learn you don't have to fall in love with every girl you f—um, sleep with. And stop frowning at me. I thought you'd like being up close to the chutes so you can take your little notes."

"Not if it's going to make everyone think I'm sleeping with you," Jenna hissed.

She noted that Mustang couldn't control his grin at her merely mentioning sex with him. "Ah, so that's the problem. Maybe this will help. I have never ever in my entire riding career left a VIP ticket for any woman I've had sex with. That make you feel any better?"

"Sadly, yes." Jenna laughed at herself. "I'm sorry. I'm being ridiculous. It was incredibly nice and sweet of you to think of me."

Mustang tipped his cowboy hat charmingly with one hand. "Why, thank you, ma'am. I do try. I'm glad you got the ticket. I told the girl to look for a beautiful, brunette, city girl, most likely dressed in black—" Mustang's eyes dropped to take in her black dress, "—who looked like she'd never been to a bull ride before in her life. You look great tonight, by the way."

In spite of the little flutter that began in Jenna's chest and down lower at his compliments, she scowled at his overt flirting. "My name on my credit card helped too, but thanks. So, um, where's Slade?"

"He's back getting his rope ready." At Jenna's blank stare, Mustang laughed. "We'll go over ropes and all the gear when we get to your book stuff later. Okay?"

She nodded, relieved. They were really going to help her. She'd been a little afraid they were only in this to flirt and try to get her into bed.

"I might even let you touch mine, if you're real nice." Mustang waggled his eyebrows.

Feeling bold, Jenna decided the flirting was all right with her too. "Okay, it's a date."

Mustang burst out laughing. His eyes roamed over her again before he shook his head. "Ah, man. Jenna, darlin', I better go and get myself ready before you put me in a state and I can't ride."

Jenna smiled. He was about to jump down, when she stopped him. "Mustang."

He paused, poised on the rail. "Yeah, darlin'?"

"Is it bad luck to wish you good luck?"

He grinned. "Not at all, but a big sloppy kiss is even better luck."

Shooting a glance at the wives and girlfriends surrounding her, not to mention the cameras and thousands of spectators, Jenna decided she couldn't do it even as much as she wanted to. Instead, she rolled her eyes at him. "Good luck, Mustang."

Jenna heard him still chuckling as his boots hit the ground and he strode away. Watching his nicely shaped, denim-covered butt framed by chaps until he was out of view, she sighed, knowing she didn't stand a chance. She'd be a card-carrying bimbo groupie by the end of the night. Glancing sideways at the tube-top-wearing girl nearby, Jenna decided that, as far as bimbo groupies went, at least she'd be a well-dressed one.

Chapter Eight

"I'm here with Slade Bower, currently third in the standings worldwide and second in points this championship on this, day two of the competition in Tulsa, Oklahoma. Slade, what is your strategy for tonight? Do you go into the night with the goal of catching the guys ahead of you?"

At this point in his career Slade could answer these questions in his sleep. He stood close to the female reporter so the cameraman could get them both in the frame. "Nope. I don't think about the other guys. When I leave that chute it's a competition between the bull and me. I'm just taking it one bull at a time."

"You heard it, folks. One bull at a time. Well, it sure seems to be working for you. Good luck tonight, Slade."

He tipped his hat. "Thank you, ma'am."

After finishing his interview with the reporter, Slade headed to get ready behind the chutes...and then he saw her. Right up there in the first row, seated almost next to the number one ranked bull rider's wife, was Jenna.

Slade smelled Mustang's hand in that and shook his head. He should have thought to leave a ticket for Jenna at the box office himself. *Shit.* Why the hell did it bother him that it was Mustang who had arranged for her seat and not him?

Then Mustang, the little do-gooder himself, appeared.

"Hey. Did you see where I got Jenna a seat?"

Slade scowled. "Yeah, I did."

"What's the matter with you? I thought you'd be happy I got her such a great seat. The arena was sold out except for the VIP block and a few seats in the back section."

"You didn't tell me you left her a ticket."

Mustang shrugged. "Sorry, it slipped my mind. Why don't you go talk to her?"

"Why don't you?" Suddenly, Slade felt cranky.

Mustang frowned at him. "Because I already did."

That figured. "How the hell am I supposed to concentrate in the chute knowing she's sitting that close, right behind me, taking her little notes?"

Mustang let out a noise of disgust. "Oh, come on. You know you could tune out a hurricane when you ride."

Normally that might be true, but last night Slade had spent hours reading Jenna's book in his bed, then spent the remaining hours until dawn picturing her in that bed with him.

He had finally fallen asleep and slept late into the day. His concentration still felt off, even after he'd dealt with the raging hard-on he'd woken up with. Lack of concentration was the last thing he wanted before getting on two thousand pounds of pissed-off bovine.

"What's up with you today? I thought you liked her."

"I do." That was the problem.

"Then you should be happy. Jenna showed up, just like I told you she would. All we have to do now is ride a couple of bulls—" Mustang elbowed Slade in the ribs, "—and then we get to ride her."

Slade scowled in disgust and Mustang threw his hands up in the air.

"What the hell, Slade? We get to do our two favorite things in the world, ride and fuck, both in one night, and you got that face on you again."

Slade narrowed his gaze at Mustang. "You shouldn't say shit like that."

"Like what?"

"How we get to *ride her* or *fuck her*. Dammit, Mustang. Jenna's a lady. She hears you saying shit like that and it's all over."

Mustang's eyebrows shot up to his hairline. "I know that, Slade. But she can't hear us from all the way over there."

"Just quit talking like that. Okay?"

"All right. I apologize."

Slade accepted the apology with a nod, then pointedly ignored Jenna in the stands and focused on the rookie rider in the chute. "I'm gonna go help the kid with his rope."

"Okay, Slade."

He felt Mustang still staring at him as he walked away.

"That was absolutely incredible. Slade, when that bull kept changing direction and you stayed on him anyway. And Mustang, I almost died when you jumped off and your bull came after you and tried to ram you in the butt with his horns."

Mustang grinned at Jenna. She'd been chattering about the competition the entire walk from the arena to the bar. "Don't worry, darlin'. The bullfighters were right there to save my ass. It's all good."

Jenna continued to shake her head. "Still. Jeez. If I'm this excited just from watching you, what you guys feel after a ride must be amazing."

Mustang's eyes met Slade's knowingly as he laughed at how true that statement was. The adrenaline rush was addictive and stuck with you well after the ride. Though they usually took advantage of the pent-up energy by sinking immediately into the first girl or two they could find, both cowboys had forgone that immediate post-ride sexual release for two nights in a row now. The reason was sitting, flushed, excited and incredibly tempting at the table with them.

"Yeah, it is pretty amazing," Mustang agreed. As the cocktail waitress arrived, he asked Jenna, "What ya' drinking tonight, darlin'?"

"Um, vodka and cranberry?"

"I knew she wasn't really a beer drinker," Slade mumbled so low only Mustang heard him.

He ignored Slade's crankiness and turned to the waitress. "A vodka cranberry for the lady. I'll have whatever domestic beer you've got in a bottle, and Slade?"

"Whisky, straight up, beer chaser."

"Okay." Mustang raised a brow at Slade's order, then turned back to the waitress. "That will do us for a while. Thank you, darlin'."

Jenna reached into her giant bag and dropped a credit card on the waitress' tray. "Could you make sure whatever the tab comes to at the end of the night goes on that card?"

"No. I'll pay." Mustang reached for his wallet when Jenna shook her head and spoke directly to the waitress. "Put it on my card, please."

"Sure thing. I'll be right back with the drinks and your card."

Mustang's mouth twisted at having the woman he was interested in buying his drinks. He enjoyed making Slade pay since he'd been ahead in the standings all year long, but Jenna paying was a different story. "You don't need to do that."

"And you don't need to help me with my book, but you are," she countered.

At that cue, Slade pulled the stack of rolled-up pages out of his back jeans pocket and Jenna's eyes lit up at the sight. "Did either of you get a chance to read it?"

Slade raised a brow at that question, looking almost offended. "Of course we did. We promised we would, didn't we?"

"I know. But I thought maybe you might be too busy. So? What did you think?"

She bit her lip and Mustang found he had trouble dragging his gaze away from her mouth as he answered, "It's good."

Jenna rolled her eyes. "Stop. Don't tell me it's good. Tell me what's wrong with it so I can make it better."

Slade pushed the papers closer to her. "There are a few things you might want to change. Terminology mostly. I made notes in the margins for you."

"You did? Thank you, Slade." Jenna stared at Slade, looking surprised, before she turned back to Mustang. "What did you think? And don't say it was good again."

Mustang shrugged. "I agree with what Slade wrote. He grabbed it and read it first." *Because at the time I was busy jerking off into the trailer's toilet while picturing you naked.*

Jenna flipped through the pages as the drinks arrived. Mustang noted she grabbed the straw while reading and had sucked down half the drink without even noticing. He considered catching the waitress' eye and ordering Jenna another.

"I can't thank you enough for doing this for me. You both are going into the dedication." Jenna looked up at them, smiling.

Across from Mustang, Slade downed the whisky and shook his head. "No need for that. Really."

"Yeah, it was nothing, darlin'," Mustang added.

Grabbing his beer to wash down the shot, Slade nodded. "Actually, it was a pretty good read."

Both Jenna and Mustang looked at Slade after that shocking comment, then Jenna turned that piercing gaze of hers on Mustang expectantly and he had no choice but to say something. The truth was he was far more interested in her than her book.

"Um, I liked it too."

She frowned at his answer. "You're a rotten liar, Mustang."

"Now, that is a terrible thing to say to a man." Grinning, Mustang rose from his seat. "Come on, darlin'. I like this song. Let's dance."

Mustang grabbed her hand, pulling her from the chair as she squealed. "But I can't dance to country music."

"Sure you can. Just follow me." Mustang held Jenna close against him and, with his leg braced between hers, steered her around the dance floor.

She soon got the rhythm of his motion and stopped looking so frightened, which he realized wasn't such a good thing when she decided to question him.

"You didn't like my book. I can tell."

Mustang opened his mouth to protest but she cut him off. "Really, it's okay. Bull-riding cowboys aren't exactly my target market so you're not supposed to like it. But I'd still like to know what you thought was wrong with it. Maybe I can fix it."

With a sinking feeling that if he said anything other than he loved her book it would mean he'd be alone with his hand again tonight, he went for it anyway. Honesty always was the best policy... Well, not always, but he couldn't come up with a believable lie right now with Jenna pressed up against him. "All right. Here's the thing. The story is okay."

"Just okay?"

He nodded, watching her face as he saw his chances with her fade away. He scrambled to get them back. "Yeah, but as you said, I'm not your market, right?"

Jenna agreed with a nod. "Right. What else?"

She'd stopped moving at all now, standing glued to the hardwood right there in the middle of the dance floor.

"Nothing. It was fine...good."

"Mustang, tell me." Her voice sounded a lot like his mama's did when she was unhappy with him. The sad part was, even that didn't smother his desire to take Jenna right then and there.

Shit. "All right. The sex scenes..."

Jenna let out a groan.

"I'm so sorry, darlin'. Really, the sex scenes are fine. Like you said, I'm not your usual reader."

"No, Mustang. You're right. Even the reviewers agree with you." Jenna sighed. "I think I'm in the wrong profession."

Mustang grabbed her face in both hands and made her look at him. "No. Listen. You're really a good writer. I really did like it."

"Except for the story and the sex scenes," she added with a scowl.

Mustang felt like shit. He'd single handedly destroyed this woman's self-confidence, not to mention his and Slade's chances with her for tonight. Slade was going to kill him. Glancing over at the table, Mustang realized Slade's eyes had never left them. "Come on. Let's go sit down and get you another drink."

"Sure, why not. It's my birthday and my career is going down the toilet. I might as well get drunk." She walked away from him and toward where Slade still sat watching them.

"It's your birthday?"

"Yup, and don't ask how old I am because I don't want to talk about it." Jenna sat and, ditching the straw, downed the remainder of her drink in one big gulp. As she flagged down the waitress, Slade shot Mustang a look that pretty clearly asked *what the hell just happened?*

He'd fucked up royally. That's what had happened.

Mustang shook his head and sent a warning glance to Slade to be quiet, then turned back to Jenna. "Why don't you want to talk about your birthday? You're what, like twenty-five?"

Jenna laughed bitterly. "Yeah. That's right. Twenty-five today."

When the waitress arrived, Jenna looked from Slade to Mustang. "You two still have something to drink back in your trailer?"

The bottle of beer stopped halfway to Slade's mouth at that question.

Mustang somehow found his own voice. "Yeah, we do."

"Okay." Jenna looked up at the waitress. "Can you please close out that tab? We're leaving."

"Sure. Let me just go get your receipt."

"I'll come up with you." Grabbing her bag, Jenna stood. "Be right back."

"Sure, darlin'." Mustang nodded, Jenna left with the waitress, and Slade jumped on him.

"What the hell happened out there on that dance floor?"

"I'm not quite sure." Mustang shook his head. He had done everything wrong and somehow she'd still suggested they go back to the trailer. Not about to question their good luck, Mustang downed the last of his beer. As Jenna returned, he said, "Let's go."

Before she changes her mind.

Chapter Nine

Jenna's heart pounded as she climbed the steps up into what proved to be nothing at all like she'd pictured a trailer would look. It was more like a huge luxury RV with a kitchenette, two beds, one large, one smaller and another loft area up above. There was even a toilet and a small shower.

"Wow. This is nice." Jenna had trouble diverting her eyes away from the large bed.

Her pulse raced. She was nervous, very nervous, and making conversation seemed the best way to postpone the inevitable—that being her and two cowboys she barely knew together in that big bed. But the moment she'd suggested they come back to the trailer, her decision had been made. After seeing the looks on both of their faces, she was pretty sure they knew it too.

There was no turning back now. Not that she wanted to. The internal do-I-or-don't-I debate was done—she only hoped her bravado lasted long enough for her to actually go through with it without passing out from nerves.

"I like to try to stay at hotels during the competitions, but they were all booked," Mustang explained apologetically. "On top of the bull-riding finals there's some huge romance convention in town, or so I was told."

As Mustang grinned pointedly at her, Jenna bit her lip and cringed. "Yeah, that would be the one I'm at. Sorry about that."

Mustang laughed. "Don't be. It's not your fault. Besides, Slade actually likes the trailer better anyway."

Jenna glanced at Slade, who was watching her and Mustang closely while not saying much. Actually, he wasn't saying anything, as usual. "I don't blame him for liking it. It's a nice trailer."

"Exactly how many trailers have you been in, darlin'?" Mustang raised a brow in challenge.

"Counting this one? Um, one." Jenna felt her cheeks heat.

Mustang grinned. "That's what I thought. Make yourself comfortable. I'm gonna hit the head, then get us those drinks."

After Mustang closed himself into the tiny toilet room, Slade finally spoke. "What's all this about, Jenna? Guzzling your drink at the bar. Asking to come back here to the trailer when last night you wanted nothing to do with it. You've done a total one-hundred-and-eighty-degree turnaround since yesterday. What's up?"

She considered his question and her answer very carefully. "Today's my birthday, Slade."

His head dipped once in a nod. "Happy birthday."

"It's my thirty-fifth." She tried not to wince.

Slade shrugged. "So what?"

"*So what?*" Jenna laughed. "Easy for you to say. What are you? Like twenty-five?"

"I'm turning twenty-seven next month actually. Mustang's twenty-five, though."

She rolled her eyes. "Great, that's just great. Well, at least I'm not old enough to have birthed you both."

Slade shook his head. "What does it matter? You're only as old as you feel."

"Maybe that's my problem, Slade. I *feel* old. I'm thirty-five, have no boyfriend, and I'm starting to seriously doubt my career choice. I'm not where I thought I'd be at this point in my life."

"First of all, you don't look thirty-five."

Jenna snorted. "Thanks."

"As for the rest, I don't know shit about writing or books or what plans you had for your life, but as far as the no boyfriend part... I can't say I'm unhappy about that."

She raised her gaze to meet his. "Really?"

That had been quite a revelation from the man of few words. For the first time since meeting him, Jenna really looked at Slade, without looking away this time. She stared deep into his dark eyes and saw the man beneath the stone-hard exterior.

He nodded. "Yeah. Really."

Maybe it had been the vodka and her deepening gloom over her crappy cowboy book on top of being yet another year older that had prompted Jenna to suggest going back to the trailer in the first place. But right now, it was Slade and his sincerity that made Jenna not doubt her decision one bit. She wanted this. Hell, she was pretty sure she needed this.

Jenna stepped forward and leaned toward him. There wasn't much distance between them to begin with given the size of the trailer, and now Slade was right in front of her, their bodies almost touching.

Slade was still too tall for her to reach what she wanted, until, eyes never leaving hers, he lowered his head a few inches, meeting her halfway. Tipping her head up to close that last temptingly tiny space, she touched her lips to his. She heard the sharp breath he dragged in through his nose at the contact.

As Slade's rough palms came up and cradled her face, his mouth pressed harder against hers...and then the latch on the trailer bathroom jiggled.

In the blink of an eye, Slade raised his head and took one giant step back, leaving Jenna alone with her raging hormones.

She and Slade maintained eye contact for what seemed like forever before Mustang came to stand next to them again. Jenna turned in time to see the interested look Mustang gave them both.

"Hi." Jenna smiled at him.

Mustang raised a brow and drawled out a slow, low, "Hey, darlin'." The sound sent a quiver straight through her.

Oh, boy, was she in trouble.

It was Slade who finally moved and broke the silence. "I need a drink." He went to a cabinet built into the wall of the trailer, took out a bottle of bourbon and a glass and poured himself a healthy amount. "Who else wants one?"

Mustang looked at Jenna questioningly. "I've got a beer in the fridge if you prefer."

Jenna shook her head. If she couldn't do this sober—or at least *fairly* sober—she probably shouldn't be doing it at all. Besides, this was for certain a once-in-a-lifetime event and she wanted to remember it. "Nothing for me. Thank you. I'm good."

Bottle still poised in the air, Slade waited for Mustang to shake his head no before he downed his own shot in one gulp. He poured another, then capped the bottle and put it back in the cabinet.

Mustang eyed Slade's bourbon consumption with a raised brow, before turning to Jenna. "So...you wanna go over the notes we made in your book some more?"

"No." She noticed Slade's eyes rarely left her as she answered Mustang.

Mustang ran a hand down her arm. "Why not? Because of what I said? I told you I don't know what the hell I'm talking about when it comes to romance novels. Don't listen to me."

She scowled. "No, you're right. It stinks."

"It doesn't stink. It just—"

"It doesn't matter, because even if I can come up with a better story idea and get it written before the deadline, you still said the sex sucks."

"You said the sex sucks?" Slade accused Mustang.

Looking uncomfortable, Mustang defended himself. "I didn't say that exactly."

"But it's what you meant." Jenna pouted.

"No, it wasn't." He shook his head.

She was seriously considering scrapping the entire project. In fact, after that last review and Mustang's comments on her current work, she was doubting the validity of her entire career.

But then what? If she stopped being a writer, what would she be? Sure, she designed graphics on the side to make some extra money, but her heart was in writing...or at least it used to be.

"It's okay, Mustang. It's true." Jenna sighed again. "My sex scenes are boring."

"I wouldn't say boring..." Mustang began.

"No, it's fine. That is exactly what one reviewer wrote. Boring." Jenna snorted out a bitter laugh.

Mustang ran a finger up and down her arm until she looked at him again. "Not boring. Just...two-dimensional. The mechanics are there but all the other stuff is missing."

She narrowed her eyes at him. "What other stuff?"

He grinned. "All the good stuff."

"I need a little more than that, Mustang." Jenna scowled. She felt more frustrated than she'd been in a long time. In so many ways.

"Come here." Mustang held both of his hands out to her. She hesitated, then stepped forward into his arms. He pulled her closer. "Good. Now, close your eyes."

Jenna swallowed hard and did as she was told.

She sensed Mustang moving even closer. When he spoke, he was near enough to her face she could smell the beer he'd drunk at the bar. "Tell me what you're feeling."

Nervous. Horny. All things she felt but wasn't willing to admit aloud. Maybe that wasn't what he meant. "I'm not sure what you want me to say."

"Okay, I'll go first, then it'll be your turn." Mustang took a deep breath before he spoke again. "I can smell your shampoo. Something fruity. It's nice, light. I can see the pulse pounding in your throat. Fast. Mmm. I like that I make your pulse race."

"Don't let it go to your head," she managed to say.

He laughed. "Don't worry. I won't. Okay, what else? I can feel you shaking a little bit—I like that too. And your lip gloss..." His tongue tickled her lips and her eyes flew open at the contact. He pulled back just a bit. "It tastes like berries. See, darlin'? Smell, sight, touch, taste. That's what's missing in your book. Sex is more than just body parts."

Jenna felt her lower parts heat. She was so aroused at this point if he even touched her she would come right there on the spot. This cowboy ten years her junior, most likely a player who had a different girl in his bed each night, knew more about not just sex but sensuality than she did.

She glanced over to where Slade still stood silently watching them, glass in hand, a tempting erection clearly outlined in his jeans. Jenna swallowed hard and looked back at Mustang as he spoke to her again.

"Now your turn, darlin'. Close your eyes."

Jenna frowned. "You were allowed to keep your eyes open."

Mustang grinned down at her from so close his impressive hard-on pressed into her hip. Judging by the physical evidence, it seemed the arousal was equally spread among the three of them.

As she fought the urge to reach down and touch Mustang and feel what had inspired his name, he nodded his head. "Yes, I did keep my eyes open, but I'm better at this than you are. You need all the help you can get. You can skip the sight part and just do the other senses. Now, eyes closed."

With a scowl, Jenna let her lids shut. Mustang's hand moved from her arm for a moment, then returned, right before a second hard body pressed close against her back and another pair of arms slid around to envelop her from behind.

Slade. He laid two large hands firmly upon her body, pressing one very low over her quivering stomach, and the other slightly higher, just below her breast.

"What do you feel, darlin'?" Mustang whispered, his breath warming her throat where it touched even as a shiver ran through her.

Heart pounding, Jenna took a deep breath and let it out slowly. "I can feel your breath, warm against my skin, tickling my throat."

Jenna sensed Mustang smile. "Good. What else?"

"I can feel Slade's heart beating against my back. He smells like a mix of whisky and something else, something fresh and clean. It's either soap or deodorant maybe. I like it. And I feel him...his...you know...pressing into me."

Slade drew in a sharp breath. She'd give anything to reach back and touch him. All of him. Jenna satisfied herself with laying her one hand over his and, making the boldest move she'd ever taken, guided it up and over her breast. He released a shaky burst of air, then Mustang's voice interrupted her thoughts.

"What else, darlin'?" Mustang prompted her again.

This is it. Now or never. Jenna took the plunge and let one hand stray down between them, pausing in the vicinity of his erection.

"I can feel you against my hip. You're hard..." she swallowed, "...and big." Not circus-freak big, which is kind of what she had been afraid of when contemplating this threesome, but definitely bigger than the average man.

Mustang's deep laugh vibrated through her. So did his voice, low and husky as his mouth hovered near her face. "Ah, darlin', you are right about that. I am both. Very. You think you can handle it?"

"Please. I'm not one of your eighteen-year-olds. I've got toys under my bed bigger than you." Jenna put on an exaggerated scowl, playing with him.

Mustang's deep chuckle reverberated through them both. "Good to hear, darlin'."

Torn between leaning into Mustang or back against Slade, she let out a satisfied groan when they both pressed closer to her.

She opened her eyes again just as Mustang's mouth was upon hers, his tongue taking no time to breach her lips. Jenna welcomed the kiss, then let her hand roam where it had wanted to go before, all the way down to trace the tempting outline of him within his jeans while he pressed hard against her.

Behind her, Slade's hands set in motion. While the one that cupped her breast began to work the now-hardened nipple through the fabric of her dress, the other headed in the opposite direction, down to lift the hem and stroke the bare skin of her thigh.

As Mustang's mouth consumed hers, Slade's warm breath tortured the whorls of her ear. Slade's fingers lifted her dress further and found the edge of her panties, then slid inside them. Jenna braced her hands against Mustang's chest for support as Slade hit the spot she needed him to and her knees went weak.

Breathing as fast as she was, Mustang broke the kiss. He reached down and grabbed the bottom of her dress, already held up around her hips by Slade.

"This needs to come off. I wanna see you." Mustang raised the garment slowly up and over her head.

She drew in a shaky breath as, somewhere past the haze of pleasure Slade was causing with just the tip of one finger on her clit, typical female thoughts assaulted her. What would they think when they saw her naked? The mushy roundness that had recently appeared on her formerly flat belly drove her crazy. And would her breasts measure up to the perky eighteen-year-olds' she'd seen in the audience eyeing her two cowboys all night?

In spite of all that, Jenna didn't protest Mustang's undressing of her. She'd envisioned this moment, though the reality was way more intense than the fantasy had been back in the hotel room when she'd chosen her nicest bra and underwear to wear tonight just in case.

Mustang let out a long, slow breath. "Damn. You are a sight."

Jenna was sure that was true, in nothing but black cowboy boots, a black lace bra and a pair of matching panties, which currently had Slade's hand inside the front of them.

He'd taken a step back while Mustang slipped the dress over her head, but Slade had gone immediately back to work, in earnest now. He zeroed right back in with incredible precision and found the spot guaranteed to make her knees buckle with one sure stroke.

Jenna let out a gasp when his finger connected with her clit again. She leaned back against the hard wall of chest behind her, reaching one hand up to hold Slade's head in place. She wanted to keep him from ever leaving that oh-so-sensitive spot on her neck his lips now tantalized while his hand tortured her down below.

As the roughened fingers of his one hand rolled the tip of her breast through the lace of her bra, Slade's touch between her legs sped faster, harder, and Jenna's heartbeat and breathing kept pace. She let her head loll back against him.

In front of her, Mustang trailed one finger tenderly down her cheek. She opened her eyes and saw him smile.

"I'm going to enjoy watching you come, darlin'."

Jenna didn't have the opportunity or the wits to respond to that before he bent and pulled her panties down over her boots, all the way to her ankles. She somehow managed to step out of them without toppling over.

Aching to be filled, Jenna purposely left her legs farther apart than they had been. As if he could sense what she needed, Mustang slid one finger into her quivering insides. He hit upon a spot that made Jenna's breath catch in her throat, eliciting a feral groan on his part.

Mustang worked that spot relentlessly while at the same time her clit swelled in response to Slade's ministrations. The combination of sensations nearly took her off her feet.

Slade's free arm abandoned her breast and wrapped tightly around her before she was in real danger of collapsing.

"Don't worry. I've got you." Slade's voice close to her ear, so deep and gentle, sent her that one last step over the edge. He did have her. They both did. Inexplicably, she trusted Slade, just as she trusted Mustang, so she let herself go totally for the first time in a long time.

As she struggled to keep her eyes open, she noticed Mustang's gaze never left her face. Slade's mouth still roamed her neck as the spasms began deep inside her. Overwhelmed, she erupted.

Unable to control any part of her body any longer, her eyelids squeezed shut and she came long, hard and loud, pressed between the two cowboys she'd met a mere twenty-four hours before. Somehow, that was okay.

Chapter Ten

Slade held on tighter, enjoying the weight of Jenna slumped against him as her orgasm slowed to a stop and she tried to catch her breath.

Deciding to give her a break for a few minutes, he left her swollen clit alone and moved that hand up to cup one lace-covered breast. They were real and perfect. Slade found he couldn't get enough of touching them, or her.

He was in no hurry to move the arm wrapped around her middle, though. It still very happily held her half-naked body tightly to him. The pressure of her against his hardened cock was nice. Being inside her, hopefully very soon, would be even nicer.

Slade was about to take steps to make that wish a reality when Jenna said, "Oh my God, Mustang. What was that you did to me?"

Mustang trailed one finger down her stomach and Slade felt Jenna's muscles jump.

"No wonder you have problems with writing your little sex scenes, darlin', if you've never had an orgasm before."

Jenna smacked at Mustang's hand. "Don't touch me there. My belly is fat. And I've had orgasms before. I mean, what did you do inside me?"

Mustang grinned broadly at that question and continued to move his hand down to between Jenna's thighs. "You are anything but fat, and that, darlin', was your G-spot. You liked that, did you?"

Slade couldn't see from behind her, but judging by the way Jenna's body jerked, Mustang had slipped a finger or two inside her again to illustrate his point. Jenna gasped as Mustang obviously located the spot in question for a second time.

She released a shuddering breath. "I thought the G-spot was a myth."

Mustang raised a brow at her. "Does *that* feel like a myth to you?"

Jenna leaned harder against Slade's chest. "No." Her voice wavered when she answered.

Mustang grinned wickedly. "Well, okay then."

Slade had watched the exchange between Mustang and Jenna for longer than he should have considering how badly he needed to sink himself into this woman.

Enough already. Jenna began to tremble from what Mustang was doing to her. If she came again, it should be with Slade's cock inside her, not Mustang's damn fingers.

"Not that this conversation isn't fascinating, but right now I have some unfinished business to take care of."

Jenna's only protest was a surprised squeak when Slade scooped her up into his arms and carried her to the biggest of the beds. With Jenna lying on her back in nothing but boots and bra and looking insanely tempting, Slade quickly kicked off his own clothes and kneeled naked between her legs.

Being helpful for once, Mustang pulled a strip of condoms from the drawer and tossed it to Slade before settling himself in the chair with a bottle of lube, giving Slade and Jenna some space.

Maybe it was selfish, but Slade liked that this first time with Jenna would be just him and her alone.

Alone. He caught sight of Mustang in the nearby chair, belt unbuckled, jeans unzipped, stroking his already-lubed cock and amended his initial opinion. He and Jenna weren't alone at all, but at least it would be only him who made Jenna come this time.

Needing her badly, Slade allowed himself only a moment to enjoy her sweet mouth as he kissed her breathless before breaking away from the magic of her lips. He didn't escape the headiness of that kiss though, no matter how short it had been. Her mouth had gotten him so crazy he needed to taste more of her and slid down her body to settle between her legs.

She spread her thighs for him. He dipped his head low and took a long, slow taste of heaven as she gasped at his touch. Her clit peeked out at him, all pink and beautiful. Slade ran first his tongue, then his teeth over it. She jerked above him and he smiled before lifting her hips with his hands and burying his tongue deep within her.

Her body trembled, and getting his head back on straight, Slade remembered how badly he needed to be inside her. He tortured her for a few more minutes, right to the brink of another orgasm, before he rose up on his knees, covered himself quickly and laid his body over hers. He slid into Jenna, who he knew firsthand would be hot, wet and more than ready for him.

Jenna's breath caught in her throat and her eyes drifted shut as he entered her. Then those beautiful eyes were open again, staring up at him with a look of amazement.

Slade was pretty amazed himself. As her hands roamed his skin, leaving trails of goose bumps in their wake, he realized it had been a while since he'd taken a woman face-to-face. It had been an even longer time since he'd wanted to see a woman's face as he loved her. He desperately wanted to watch Jenna's features react to every movement he made inside her now.

Slipping one arm beneath her hips, Slade angled her pelvis so he hit the sweet spot inside her with every thrust. Mustang wasn't the only one who knew how to rub Jenna the right way, and Slade intended to prove that then and there. Judging by her gasping breaths and the way her nails dug into the skin of his back, he was doing a good job.

Buried inside her, Slade kissed her lips, nibbling the lower one he'd watched her bite countless times since he'd met her. He stopped kissing her only long enough to enjoy the sight of her adorable flushed cheeks and sex-brightened eyes.

She cried out his name and a shudder ran through him at the sound of it. He both heard and felt her gearing up to come again, and when her muscles gripped him he thought he'd died and gone to heaven.

"Ah, Jenna. Yes." Slade held still and enjoyed every single pulse of her body surrounding his.

He stayed deeply inside her as the spasms finally slowed and stopped.

Slade realized the error he'd made when he had to thrust hard and fast and for far too long to finally make himself come. Too much hard liquor always did that to him and, though he never wanted to leave the warmth of Jenna's body, he was afraid he'd make her sore. Besides, Mustang was still waiting his turn.

For the first time, Slade felt his stomach twist at the thought of Mustang sliding in right after him. Maybe Mustang would settle for a blowjob instead. The image of Jenna and Mustang like that didn't make Slade feel much better as he imagined how nice it would be to have Jenna's mouth wrapped around his own cock instead of Mustang's.

With a sigh, Slade could delay no longer. He rolled off Jenna. She was still panting when Mustang wasted no time moving right in.

"That took fucking forever," Mustang mumbled, before lying on the other side of Jenna. "Hey there, darlin'."

She smiled back at him weakly. "Hi."

"You doing okay?"

"Yeah."

Mustang slid one hand between her gorgeous thighs and she drew in a sharp breath.

A wrinkle appeared between those beautiful eyes, bringing a frown to Slade's own face. "What wrong?"

"I'm just a little sensitive. You took a long time to...um, finish." She blushed deeper and couldn't say the word come.

Slade felt his own cheeks color. "I know. I'm sorry."

"It's okay, I was just afraid I did something wrong."

"No. Of course you didn't." Slade glanced up and saw Mustang scowling at him.

"Okay." Her voice sounded so small and vulnerable.

Great. Now Jenna felt like a failure all because he took so long to come. Slade flopped over onto his back next to her, staring at the ceiling.

Slade turned his head in time to see Mustang crawl from his perch on the very edge of the bed to lie between Jenna's legs. Mustang traced lines up and down her stomach with his fingers, bringing goosebumps to her skin.

"It's nothing you did, darlin'. Slade here can't finish when he drinks bourbon, or too much beer even. It always happens. Nothing to do with you at all."

"Always?"

"Yup."

"How do you know?"

Mustang leaned forward to pop one nipple out of her bra and nibble on it before he answered. "Because I'm usually there, darlin'."

The moment the words left Mustang's mouth and Slade saw the look on Jenna's face, Slade knew Mustang should have kept his mouth shut. He grinned at the stricken look on Mustang's face when he made the same realization.

"Exactly how often do you two do this together?" The fire in Jenna's voice made Slade smile.

With one firm shove of her tiny hand against his shoulder, Mustang was no longer enjoying the taste of Jenna, much to Slade's enjoyment.

Mustang turned to Slade for help but all Slade was willing to do was give him the you-did-this-yourself, you-dumb-ass look. As if Slade was going to get Mustang out of the mess he'd made. Slade was too busy reveling in the fact that he'd gotten to have Jenna, even if it did upset her because he'd taken so long to finish, which was his own damn whisky-drinking fault. In the meantime, Mustang was the one with the dick hard enough to hammer nails, and the now pissed off woman between his legs who looked like she wasn't about to help him out with it.

Slade glanced at Jenna's face and found her impatiently awaiting Mustang's answer to her question about how often they shared women.

"Um... Well, you see..." Mustang turned to Slade again and this time, he complied.

"Every chance we can get," Slade answered for them both.

Now it was Mustang's turn to give Slade the you-dumb-ass look. Slade grinned and shrugged. Glancing back at Jenna to see her reaction to that little tidbit, he found her frowning.

"Um... You okay with that, darlin'?" Mustang asked.

She sighed deeply. "I guess I would have been stupid to assume I was the first."

The expression on her face said she'd assumed just that.

Slade waited for Mustang to break out one of his usual lines. *You're the best. Yes, there have been others, but you're special.* Instead, he shocked the hell out of Slade and opted for the truth.

"It doesn't matter who's been here before you, or even who'll be here after you. Right now, I want you so bad I can't even remember another one of those girls. Hell, I can barely even remember my own mama's name."

Then Mustang kissed her long and hard, and she kissed him back, her hips rising slightly off the bed as Mustang's hand strayed between her thighs.

"You feeling up to doing this, darlin'? I want to be inside you more than anything else in the world, but we can get creative if you're too sore."

Slade watched Jenna's tiny hand reach down and grasp Mustang's erection as she smiled shyly. "I think I'll be okay. I kinda want to give it a try."

Mustang grinned. "That's fine with me."

Mustang slid one leg between hers while Jenna more than willingly let him, and Slade felt a fist grab his heart and squeeze.

Chapter Eleven

"Jenna? *Hello*. Earth to Jenna."

Jenna looked up to find Barb waving a hand in front of her face.

"Huh? Did you say something?"

"Um, yeah. I asked you a question. Where is your head today? You're totally zoned out."

Her head was where the rest of her wanted to be, back in the trailer with the two cowboys. Jenna shook the images of the night before from her spinning brain. "Sorry. I'm just tired."

"I'd say. You look like you didn't sleep at all last night. You okay?"

"Yeah, fine. You know how I am. I don't sleep well if I'm not at home in my own bed."

In fact, Jenna hadn't even made it back to her hotel room last night. There'd barely been time after Slade and Mustang had dropped her back at the hotel that morning to shower and get to her first session, forget about catch a nap. Jenna sure as hell couldn't tell Barb she'd been awake having sex with two pro bull riders in their trailer in the parking lot of the sports arena for most of last night.

With that thought, the memories again flooded her mind and the rest of her body. Mustang pushing his very impressive erection into her. How she lied through her teeth and teased him afterward that he wasn't that big after all. Then, after an hour or two of exhausted sleep between the two hot, hard male bodies, waking up in the dawn light to discover Slade sliding into her while Mustang snored beside them.

Slade had loved her slowly, silently, until they both shook with orgasms as his mouth covered hers in a deep kiss. She'd felt strangely sad and empty after he finally pulled out and slipped from the bed to use the toilet. Slade's exit from the bed, or maybe the sound of the bathroom door closing, had woken Mustang, who apparently was as ready again after his short sleep as Slade had been.

In the midst of the ballroom, Jenna shifted in her chair and felt the tug of soreness in muscles she hadn't been aware existed and body parts that were sadly not used often enough.

She let out a sigh and noticed Barb watching her with concern.

"Luckily we aren't here for much longer. Then you can go home to New York and get some rest."

Jenna nodded even as her stomach twisted at the thought of leaving. She'd go back to New York. Slade and Mustang would go... She didn't know where, but she was sure of one thing, wherever they went there'd be plenty of willing females. The guys would forget all about her. Unfortunately, she wouldn't be able to put either of them out of her mind as easily.

The wait staff circled their table like sharks and Jenna noticed they'd cleared everyone else's lunch plates except hers, which remained barely touched. As she poked at her chicken Caesar salad half-heartedly Barb whipped out her conference itinerary.

"So we have the book signing for the rest of the afternoon and then the awards dinner after that. Ugh. Did you see who's up for Author of the Year?"

Jenna had seen, all right. She'd been green with envy the day that list had been posted online. She groaned. "Yeah. Lizzie."

Lizzie Lundgren. Her arch nemesis. Okay, maybe that was overly dramatic, but the woman's overnight success as an author never failed to raise the acid level in Jenna's stomach.

Barb's mouth twisted into a grimace. There was no love lost between Barb and Lizzie either. "Yup. Oh, well. At least it will be an early night. There's nothing planned for after the awards."

Jenna nodded absently, her mind obsessing about what Slade and Mustang would be doing while she was begrudgingly applauding for the award winners over her prime rib, baby potatoes, green beans and strawberry shortcake, or whatever typical conference meal the hotel had planned to feed them that evening.

The two bull riders wouldn't be riding bulls, of that Jenna was certain because they'd told her they had today off from competition so all the riders could rest up for the final round the next night. The question was what, or rather whom, would they be riding?

Never let it be said that Jenna wasn't up for a little old-fashioned jealousy, whether it be in her personal or her professional life.

"A few of us were talking about going out after dinner. Maybe find a townie bar, check out the local color. You up for it?"

Sad and one step away from outright pouting over thoughts of Slade and Mustang out in a bar checking out some eighteen-year-olds, Jenna shook her head. "I think I'll be heading to bed early."

"Oh, come on. We won't be out late."

Jenna took a drink of her complimentary unsweetened iced tea and grimaced at the flavor, reaching for the bowl of sweetener in the middle of the table. "But we all have that publisher's breakfast mixer bright and early tomorrow morning."

"Yeah, so I see. Right back here in the good old Grand Ballroom, which is where we'll be eating dinner tonight too." Barb consulted the itinerary one last time, then shoved it into her bag. "I really do think it would be a shame for you to see nothing but this damn ballroom before we leave Tulsa. Don't you wanna absorb some true Oklahoma culture? Maybe find a cowboy or two?"

At that Jenna nearly choked on her second sip of tea.

If Barb noticed Jenna's reaction, she didn't comment on it. Instead, she glanced around the room. "I wonder if one of the wait staff knows where there is a real dive. You know, the kind of bar where a pitcher of beer costs like nothing and the men all wear cowboy hats and dance to whatever country song is on the jukebox."

Jenna bit her tongue so she didn't accidentally spew out the fact she knew exactly where such a bar existed. Then the jealous, possessive wheels in her head began to turn. She pictured Mustang's cocky grin as he made some cowgirl laugh. Jenna imagined Slade's dark, intense stare focused on another woman and she couldn't stand it anymore.

A plan began to form. Why couldn't she just show up at the bar? It was a free country. If Slade and Mustang happened to be there and Jenna happened to look amazing in her dress for the awards ceremony, so what?

Before she could stop herself, her lips were moving and words coming out. "Um. I heard about a bar like that."

"Really? From who?"

"Um, from my cousin. Remember? The one who lives near here. Well, not too near, but near enough."

"I remember. That was where you were last night instead of at the Vampire Ball after-party. It was your cousin's daughter's birthday or something."

"Mmm hmm. That's the one. Anyway, her husband told me about this bar." *Shit.* Jenna better quit while she was ahead before she got caught lying. But what could she have said that morning over breakfast when Barb had questioned her absence at the after-party? She sure as hell couldn't tell her the truth about where she'd been. Sleep deprived and still glowing from morning sex, Jenna had been lucky she'd come up with any story at all.

"Great. Let's go there then. This is going to be so much fun. I never get to go out at home."

Jenna tried to mimic Barb's glee as her own heart began to pound in anticipation of seeing Slade and Mustang again. When exactly had Jenna lost her mind over these two cowboys? She'd like to say she could peg the exact moment at sometime between her third and fourth orgasms. She sure as hell wouldn't mind going for a few more of those tonight. Unfortunately, she feared orgasms were only a very small part of her attraction to the two men.

That thought was interrupted when Jenna's cell phone started ringing. She glanced down at it, saw Astrid's name on the caller ID and hit the silent button.

Astrid would want to know what had happened last night. Jenna couldn't admit to herself what had gone on in that trailer. How was she supposed to admit it to Astrid? Jenna was sure of only one thing. She wanted it to happen again.

With a quick text to Astrid explaining she couldn't talk now and would call later, Jenna wove one more lie into her ever-growing web.

Chapter Twelve

With a stretch of stiff muscles, accompanied by the popping of joints and a groan, Slade rolled over in the narrow bed and squinted at the clock on the other side of the trailer.

Peering through the dim light, Slade noted Mustang still sprawled unconscious across the bigger of the trailer's two beds. Mustang had spent the night as busy as Slade had, and in the exact same way...with Jenna in that big bed. Slade tried not to think too much about that.

The time displayed on the digital readout told him it was already late afternoon, but Slade couldn't regret sleeping the day away, especially considering the reason why. He'd gladly sleep all day every day if it were because he'd been up making love to Jenna most of the night.

Damn. Just the thought of Jenna had Slade aroused again.

Really good memories of her hit him. Her soft sighs when he had slid into her early that morning. The feel of her beneath his hands.

Then there were the images of her that had nothing to do with sex. The way she'd giggle when Mustang made a stupid joke, or how she would listen intently to everything Slade said, as if he was the most interesting person in the world.

Shit. He had to stop himself from thinking about Jenna anymore because on top of being hard as a rock, he also really had to piss. Time to get up and take care of at least one of his current bodily needs.

Stifling another groan, Slade rose from the bed at about the pace of an eighty-year-old man, or that of a bull rider who had broken more bones over the course of his career than he could count.

On the way back from the bathroom, Slade's stomach growled loudly and he realized he'd have to deal with that need soon too.

Mustang laughed from the bed. "Yeah, I could eat too. But damn, I'm still tired."

Crawling back into his own bed for just another minute or two, Slade had to agree. "Yeah. Me too. Think they'll deliver a pizza to the trailer?"

Mustang laughed again. "Might be worth a try. I could use another hour's sleep though. Fucking all night and half the morning sure does take a lot out of a man."

Slade scowled. "Shut up, Mustang. I hate when you say shit like that."

Mustang sighed. "All right, what'd I do wrong now?"

"Never mind," Slade mumbled.

"No. Not *never mind*. I can see you making a face over there. You're pissed at me for something."

"I am not. Go back to sleep."

"No. Tell me what the hell is wrong or I'll keep asking until you do...all day," Mustang glanced at the clock himself, "or all night long if I have to."

Slade had no doubt, so he gave in. "I just don't like you using that word when you're talking about Jenna."

Mustang pushed himself upright to lean back against the headboard, frowning. "What word? Fucking?"

"Yes."

"You're mad because I said fucking? Are you kidding me? I use that word all the time, for everything, and so do you. What's the problem?"

"Say it as much as you want, but don't use it for what you and I did with Jenna. All right?" The more the conversation went on, the more ridiculous Slade felt for starting it. Especially when Mustang stared at him with a look of shock on his face.

"You're getting really weird lately."

"Just because I don't want you to insult Jenna? That's not weird. Go back to sleep, Mustang." Slade squeezed his eyes shut, wishing for quiet.

"That's another thing. You not only remember her name, but you actually said it while you were f—having sex with her."

Slade groaned and wished again he'd never started this. "I said her name. So what?"

"So what? You never do that. Ever. You usually can't even remember their names and if you do, you never say them during sex."

This conversation was going places Slade didn't want it to go. "Shut up, Mustang."

There was silence for a few short, peaceful moments, then it was over when Mustang's lips started flapping again.

"You kissed her too."

Slade kept his mouth glued shut, hoping Mustang would take the hint and do the same. He didn't.

"You never kiss them. And you went down on her. You never ever do that. Not in front of me, anyway."

Shit. Slade really didn't want to discuss this. "What the hell, Mustang? Are you going to analyze the way I fuck now too?"

Never slow when it came to verbal sparring, Mustang shot right back, "I thought we weren't using that word anymore, and actually, yeah, I am gonna analyze how you fuck. You faced her. You always do them from behind."

"Jesus Christ! First of all, it's freaking me out that you were watching me so damn close."

"Well, don't say it like that. I wasn't drooling over your ass or anything. I was just watching you watching her, which you did the whole time, by the way. You never took your eyes off her face and you never do th—"

"Is there a point to all of this shit?" Slade cut off Mustang's sexual recap.

"Yes, there is."

"And I'm sure you're about to enlighten me." Letting out a sigh, Slade resigned himself to the fact Mustang wasn't nearly done yet. He should have just kept his mouth shut to begin with or gone out and gotten them that damn pizza. Too late now.

From across the trailer, Mustang grinned at him. "Of course I am. The point is that you like Jenna."

"So I like her. Big deal. You do too." Slade punched his pillow into place and faced the wall, hoping it would shut Mustang up and end this conversation once and for all.

"Sure I like her. Jenna's great. That's not the point. I mean you *like* like her."

"*Like* like her." Slade rolled over and lifted himself up on one elbow to stare at Mustang in the other bed. "What, are you in fifth grade?"

"You're the one acting like you're some middle-schooler with a crush. You're so quiet you barely even talk to her, but you're always staring at her." As Slade flopped back onto the mattress with a huff, Mustang continued. "And what the hell was with all the shots of whisky last night? You know what happens to you when you—"

"Mustang, enough!" Slade growled.

"Admit to me you like her and I'll shut up."

"I seriously doubt that." How the hell could Slade admit to Mustang what he couldn't even admit to himself? "Just go back to sleep."

Mustang laughed. "Okay, Romeo."

Then thankfully, there was quiet, except for the incredibly loud thoughts careening through Slade's head and the echo of Mustang's observation.

You like Jenna.

Yeah, Slade realized he did, and his only thought after admitting that to himself was, *Shit.*

Chapter Thirteen

As the taxi pulled up in front of the now-familiar bar and the four authors crammed inside threw money at the driver, Jenna began to fully realize her error in suggesting they come here.

What if Slade and Mustang were inside? They would most likely come right over and each plant a huge kiss on her right in front of her friends. Then what? She'd have to explain to her author buddies that she'd had a little cowboy threesome fantasy for herself the night before. No way could she do that. She would just have to get to them first and tell them to play it cool and pretend they'd just met her.

As Jenna slid out of the cab and pulled the hem of her dress down, she realized that scenario was the best case. The worst case, and far more likely, would be that by this late hour the two cowboys were already deeply engrossed in picking up another woman in that bar.

So there Jenna stood, staring at the door, too frightened to open it, afraid to face what might be inside.

She nearly spun around and ran after the cab until Barb opened the door and Ann and Megan, the other two authors behind her, pretty much carried her through the entrance. Everyone in their party except Jenna was enthusiastic to get inside. They now knew there would be cowboys there after Barb had read aloud the message on the flashing arena sign across the street about the bull-riding competition. Jenna's companions were not disappointed by the sea of wall-to-wall cowboy hats they found within.

Apparently, a day off from competition meant every bull rider in the event had nothing else to do but come to the bar. Heart lodged firmly in her throat, Jenna quickly scanned the room and breathed a sigh of mixed relief and disappointment. Dozens of eyes looked in their direction, but the two pairs she sought specifically weren't there.

Jenna considered the reason why Slade and Mustang were conspicuously absent. Obviously they'd already selected a tasty tidbit from the buckle-bunny buffet and were enjoying her back in the trailer.

Jenna felt her heart squeeze even as Barb tugged her hand. Her friend pulled her through the crowd toward a table which, while in her self-pity reverie, Jenna hadn't noticed their two companions claim in the far corner. The same table she had shared with Slade and Mustang that first night.

The neon blue beer sign still hung where it had, except now it illuminated four city girls rather than the two bull riders who'd made love to her not even twenty-four hours before. That thought caused a twisting of desire low in Jenna's belly, while at the same time she felt nauseated as she again wondered who they were with now.

A cocktail waitress appeared, the same one who had served them the night before. Jenna bit her lip, praying the woman wouldn't mention her presence for three nights in a row, or the fact she'd left with the same two cowboys for two nights.

"How about a pitcher of beer, ladies?"

Nods of assent followed Barb's suggestion.

"What do you have on tap? Anything brewed locally?" Barb asked.

That question got a raised eyebrow from the waitress. "We've got Bud on tap. That's it."

"Okay. Bud it is then, and four glasses."

Jenna smiled to herself, knowing from experience they'd be getting four plastic cups, not glasses. She may be out of place here, but at least she had some experience under her belt. The other three were total fish out of water.

"Look at all the cute cowboys." Ann looked around wide-eyed.

"Yeah, and they're all about the same age as my son," Megan commented.

"They kind of have to be young to ride bulls. The oldest pro bull rider in competition is thirty-eight."

Jenna glanced around and realized all eyes were upon her.

"How do you know all this?" Ann's question had Jenna speechless for a moment.

"She's writing a cowboy book," Barb supplied.

Jenna nodded her head, thankful for Barb's explanation. She'd forgotten she'd told Barb the contemporary she was writing had a cowboy theme. "Yup. I've been doing my research. You'd be amazed what you can find on the Internet."

Megan nodded. "Oh yeah. You should see all the stuff I found on treatments for insanity during the Regency period in England."

With that, the conversation turned to what it always did when authors got together, to whatever books they were working on.

Jenna breathed a sigh of relief that the spotlight was off her and took the time to look around the bar. Resigned to the fact that Slade and Mustang weren't there, it somehow made her feel better that she could identify some of the riders from the competition.

She noted one cowboy staring at her. He caught her eye and, before she could avert her gaze, he was smiling and heading in her direction.

Wide-eyed, she watched as he made a beeline to their table and tipped his hat.

All conversation stopped again as the three romance authors, as eager for a good story in life as on paper, watched the action between Jenna and the young bull rider.

He gave her a, "Howdy, ma'am" that in any other situation would have charmed the pants off her. If he wasn't a child and if she wasn't already half in love with Slade and Mustang.

"Um, hi."

"I recognized you from the stands and I just thought I'd say hey."

Jenna saw the interested glances of her friends. "Um, I'm sorry. You must be mistaken."

"Last night. You were seated with the riders' wives and girlfriends... You know, right behind the chutes."

"Um, no. Sorry. Must have been somebody else."

Strangely, his face brightened. "Really? Hmm. Well, I apologize for the mistake. Would you like to dance?"

With another look at the women at the table, Jenna was torn about what to do. Go with him to the dance floor so at least he was away from her friends and couldn't out her? Or say no thank you and hope he went away.

Apparently she had no choice in the matter, because her friends practically flung her from the table while at the same time the young bull rider grabbed her hand and led her out to the dance floor.

Before Jenna knew it, she was encased in his arms and spinning around the hardwood, exactly where she had been the night before, but in Mustang's embrace. When exactly had her life gotten so strange?

"So, I have to admit something to you. I'm glad I made a mistake about you being at the arena last night."

Her writer's curiosity raised, Jenna couldn't help herself and asked, "Why is that?"

He grinned charmingly, his blue eyes twinkling. "Because if that had been you in the VIP section, that would mean you were with one of the other riders."

Jenna sighed as she evaluated if this kid was old enough to legally even be in the bar and drink. "Listen, um, what was your name?"

"Chase." He smiled again.

"Hi, Chase. I'm Jenna."

Chase dipped his head once in greeting. "Jenna, that's a beautiful name. It fits you perfectly. A beautiful name for a beautiful woman."

Damn, the kid had all the bar-pickup lines down already. She ignored his flirting and got back to the issue at hand, the fact that Chase recognized her from the competition. What if he brought up again how he thought he'd seen her the night before and the other authors started to ask questions? He could expose her to her friends as a liar and a sneak, not to mention a slut if you added in the two cowboys she'd had sex with.

"Listen, Chase. I'm going to tell you a secret and I'm going to ask you not to tell anyone else. Can you do that?"

"Sure." He looked tickled that she was willing to share a confidence with him.

"I was at the arena last night but I lied to my friends back there and told them I was somewhere else."

Chase frowned and glanced back at the table full of women. "Why?"

Sighing, Jenna decided to try something new for a change and told him the truth—most of it anyway. "It's kind of complicated, but long story short, I'm a writer."

"Wow. Have I read anything you've written?"

"I doubt it. But the point is, it is an extremely competitive business and, for certain reasons, I didn't want one particular author to know that I was at the competition last night researching my book."

Lizzie Lundgren's book that had landed her on the best-seller list had been a cowboy book. With her sitting at the table at breakfast when Barb had asked where Jenna had been the night before, not to mention the trailer sex, Jenna had had to lie. She wasn't about to let Lizzie know real live cowboys were camped out a short car ride from their hotel.

Chase nodded. "Because she might steal your idea."

Jenna smiled. "Yeah, something like that. So you understand why I can't let any of my friends back there know that you saw me last night?"

Chase glanced back at the table of women, who were no doubt still watching them like hawks, then leaned in conspiratorially. "Don't worry. Your secret is safe with me."

He didn't lean back after the whisper, but stayed with his head pressed against hers. He was taller than her, but with his head tipped down, Chase's sandy curls tickled her face.

She might have been tempted, in another lifetime where she was ten years younger and not still sore from a night of having sex with not one, but two of this kid's fellow bull riders. But as things stood, Jenna was old and, in spite of last night's threesome, not a loose enough woman to sleep her way through the ranks of the top bull riders, even though Chase was absolutely adorable and obviously interested in her.

It was up to Jenna to lean her head back so she could point the obvious issue out to him. "Chase. How old are you?"

He grinned proudly. "Twenty-one today, ma'am."

Twenty-one. *Jeez.* Jenna stifled a groan at that revelation.

He should only know that the constant ma'am-ing was not helping his case with her one bit. "Chase. Listen. I am way too old for you."

"Heck no, you're not. I like women a few years older than me."

A few. She controlled a burst of bitter laughter at his description of her. But it did explain why he was bothering with her and not one of the young girls scattered around the bar giving Jenna the evil eye for dancing with him. She allowed herself another glance at them, and if they were old enough to legally drink, she'd eat Chase's hat.

Jenna directed her focus back onto Chase, who was obviously having a little younger-man-older-woman-Mrs.-Robinson fantasy for himself, so the age issue wasn't going to dissuade him. She'd have to try another tactic.

"I'm not exactly available, Chase." That wasn't really a lie either. No, she wasn't dating Slade or Mustang by any stretch of the imagination, but they were the only ones she was interested in at the moment. That made her unavailable.

Even if they were probably with some other woman. The resurgence of that thought twisted her gut nicely.

"Is he here with you now?" Chase looked around the bar, knowing full well she'd walked in with three women and no men. Every person in there had turned to watch their entrance.

"No." Unfortunately.

She hated the thought of where they were and what they were doing.

Chase smiled sweetly. "Then don't worry about it. It's just a dance, Jenna. Make a cowboy happy on his birthday and give him just one dance. Okay?"

Feeling a bit relieved, Jenna returned his smile. "Okay."

As Chase steered her expertly around the dance floor to the strains of some broken-heart country song, she let herself relax and enjoy the dance and the attention. Who knew when she'd get such unfailing male devotion again once she left Tulsa?

Where were these kind of guys when she was growing up? Certainly not in the suburbs of New York. Apparently, she should have come to Tulsa years ago.

"In case I don't get a chance later, I just wanted to thank you for the dance, Jenna."

"You're welcome. It's the least I can do for your twenty-first birthday." She smothered a cringe at the number she hadn't been able to claim in a long, long time.

"Maybe I can get just one little kiss too? You know, for my birthday." Chase raised his brow expectantly and treated Jenna to a sweetly naughty, cherubic grin that only made her laugh.

"Don't push it, cowboy." Jenna's warning probably held less weight considering she was trying not to laugh at his creative tactics while she said it.

Chase smiled. "We'll see. I think you'll come around to my way of thinking."

Now, Jenna did laugh at him. "Oh boy, you are a persistent one."

"You have to be persistent in this business. Hey, do you know that I'm up for Rookie of the Year? There's a good chance I'll get it too, as long as I make both my rides tomorrow night."

Jenna realized she'd been hanging around this environment too long when she heard herself ask, "Rookie of the Year. Do you get a buckle for that?"

Chase grinned wider. "Yes, ma'am. I do. You're interested in buckles, are you?"

Obviously the term "buckle bunny" was familiar to even the younger riders and her interest in his pending buckle had gotten Chase's hopes up even further. Jenna laughed again at the ridiculousness of the entire situation but still didn't have it in her to totally crush his hopes.

"I'm interested in lots of things. It's one of the side effects of being a writer."

Selfish as it felt, she was really enjoying the attention. It made her disappointment about Slade and Mustang's absence, and her worries over where they were and who they were with, fade a bit. The song ended and Jenna took the opportunity to disengage herself from the arms of the kid young enough to be her biological child in certain third-world countries. "Thanks for the dance, Chase. I enjoyed it, but I better get back to my friends now."

Chase glanced back at the table and grinned. "Okay, but I think they're doing just fine without you."

Jenna followed his gaze and couldn't believe what she saw.

What was going on?

Their table was totally swamped with bull riders, and by the looks on the faces of her friends, they loved it. "How did that happen?"

Chase laughed. "What can I say? We're a welcoming group. Come on, I'll walk you back to the table."

They hadn't even gotten all the way back to the corner yet when one of the bull riders spotted them. "Hey, Chase. Did you know these women all write romance novels?"

True to the cowboy gentleman stereotype, the cowboy who'd spoken abandoned the chair he occupied and swung it behind Jenna so she could sit. Jenna couldn't remember the last time a man had given her his seat back in New York.

"That's my friend, Garret," Chase informed her. "Romances, huh? You said you were a writer, but you didn't say romance."

Jenna found herself not only seated, but also with a cup of beer. It mysteriously appeared and was shoved in her hand. Taking a gulp for lack of anything else to drink, she let the cold foam slide down her suddenly dry throat.

She looked up at Chase above her and shrugged. "Eh, you know, I like to remain mysterious."

Chase squatted down next to the chair and tipped his hat back so he could look up at her.

He laughed. "You are that, Jenna. You definitely are that. Mysterious and beautiful."

Jenna shook her head at him. "And you, Chase, are a flatterer and a flirt."

She watched another smile curve his lips and sighed while trying to ignore how good the attention felt. She wrote it off to her thirty-five-year-old psyche enjoying the attentions of a younger, okay, *much* younger man. But a little innocent flattery couldn't hurt anyone, could it?

Around her, the other three authors had never looked happier, each flanked by at least one cowboy. The one next to Barb, Garret, grabbed the now-empty pitcher. As he left to refill it at the bar, Barb leaned over close to Jenna. "Oh, my God. These are real cowboys."

Jenna laughed. "Yeah, I know."

"I mean *real*, not just guys who like to wear boots and hats," Barb amended.

Yeah, she'd noticed that distinction herself. Still laughing, Jenna raised her voice. "Barbara, this is Chase. He's competing in the bull-riding finals and he's up for Rookie of the Year."

Chase stood and tipped his hat to Barb. "Ma'am."

Jenna couldn't help but smile at Barb's expression as she looked from Jenna to Chase and back to Jenna again. If that look didn't insinuate that Jenna should go for it, she didn't know what it did say.

If only Barb knew Jenna had already gotten herself a cowboy, two in fact. That thought had Jenna glancing around the bar once more, looking for the two missing men.

Chase got pushed farther back behind her when the other cowboy returned with another two full pitchers of beer and put them on the table. Barb took that opportunity to lean in again. "Chase is adorable."

"Yeah, adorable, just like a puppy." Jenna rolled her eyes.

Barb shrugged. "So he's young. Big deal. It's not like you're going to marry him. I think you'd get more out of one night with him than that conference session you took about writing hotter sex."

"Oh my God, Barb. You are so bad." Jenna felt her face heat. She dared a glance in Chase's direction and saw him watching her and smiling. Yeah, odds were good he knew he was the subject of the conversation, which had Jenna's cheeks reddening even further, she was sure.

"When else can you be bad, Jenna? Come on. What happens at the romance writers' convention in Tulsa, stays at the romance writers' convention in Tulsa."

Jenna seriously doubted that was true, considering the notorious gossips attending the conference.

Barb's cowboy finally finished pouring beer for the table, including Jenna, she noted as she glanced at her almost overflowing cup. Jenna was happy when he then went back to focusing on Barb, which meant that Barb didn't have the time to focus on Jenna's sex life any further.

She felt a hand on her shoulder right before she felt a warm breath of air tickle her ear. "You sure are cute when you blush."

Jenna felt the heat deepen and spread across her already-blazing cheeks at that comment. Chase grinned wider because of it. She raised the big plastic cup, took another huge swallow and tried to ignore Chase's attention.

As the noise level increased and the beer started to go to her head, Jenna saw close to a dozen shot glasses suddenly appear on the table. Soon she was swallowing something that burned her throat and made her cough. She grabbed her cup of beer and downed it gladly to soothe the fire of the shot.

Before she knew it, she was having difficulty walking a straight line to the bar's bathroom. In the ladies' room, Jenna wasn't so drunk she didn't think to check out how she looked in the mirror as she washed her hands. Nor did she forget to reapply her lipstick, though staying in the lines seemed to take more concentration than it should have. Running her fingers through her hair, she consulted her flushed reflection one last time and grabbed the door handle, cringing when she overestimated the weight of the door and sent it crashing into the wall.

Pretending she hadn't caused the racket, she slipped into the hallway that contained the doors to the men's and ladies' rooms as well as an ancient-looking payphone and found Chase waiting for her.

"Hey, there." He put one hand on her shoulder and smiled at her, but it wasn't in an aw-shucks-ma'am way like when he'd first approached her that night. It was in a sultry and very adult I'm-a-man-and-you're-a-woman-so-how-about-it way that twisted her stomach and parts lower.

"Hey." Her voice sounded husky in her own ears.

Chase made a point to consult the digital readout on his cell phone before he held it up for her to see. "I still have a few hours left of my birthday. There's time for you to give me that birthday kiss you promised."

Had she promised that? Between Chase's temptingly sexy lips and the alcohol, she honestly couldn't remember. When he leaned his head down so his mouth was barely a breath from hers, Jenna stopped trying to remember and instead let him close the small distance to meet her.

Things quickly became a blur as Chase's hands came up to first cup her face, then tangle in her hair. He kissed her deeper and she let him, opening her mouth when his tongue slid between her lips.

Heart pounding, she found herself pressed up against the wall by Chase's lean, hard body. She wrapped her arms around his waist as he tipped his head and kissed her harder. That slight shift of his position pressed his thigh more closely in between hers and she realized just how good that pressure felt. Too good. She wanted more. She didn't want to want more.

Jenna pulled away and broke the kiss. Chase let her, leaning his forehead against hers for just long enough to let out a satisfied moan.

"Thank you, Jenna. That was the best birthday present I've gotten in a very long time." Then he straightened up, grabbed her hand, adjusted the cocked brim of his hat and led her back to the table, where too many pairs of eyes widened and more than a few sets of eyebrows rose.

Jenna glanced at Chase and saw he was smeared in her lipstick. She shot him a quick signal to wipe his mouth as his fellow bull riders chuckled. She quickly took a moment to wipe at her own undoubtedly lipstick-smeared mouth.

Horrified, she glanced at her friends and found them grinning widely and looking as drunk as she felt. Barb raised a shot to her in salute and smiled, right before Barb's cowboy grabbed her hand, pulled her from the chair and led Barb back toward the same hallway.

Halfway across the floor, Barb turned. "What happens in Tulsa…"

"Stays in Tulsa," Megan echoed, as she was pulled giggling into the lap of a cowboy. Ann didn't answer since her mouth was suddenly occupied by the fourth cowboy.

Jenna glanced up at Chase, who shrugged, then started to massage her neck and shoulders gently. "I told you we were a welcoming bunch."

As her head lolled to the side in ecstasy, Jenna had to agree. "You can say that again."

Chapter Fourteen

Mustang leaned back in his chair and rubbed his stomach. "Ooo wee. That was good. I was so hungry my stomach was eating my backbone."

Slade mirrored Mustang and leaned back in the chair of the pizza parlor. "Yeah, but I'm thinking we probably shouldn't have eaten the whole thing."

Probably not, since a full belly could get uncomfortable. Especially for the next activity that Mustang had a hankering for. "So, you wanna hit the bar and see who's there?"

"I'm sure every bull rider in the competition will be there, since we had the day off."

"Most likely, but I wasn't talking about bull riders." Grinning suggestively, Mustang balled up his napkin, threw it onto his grease-stained paper plate and pushed the whole mess farther away from him as Slade mulled that over.

When Mustang looked up again, he saw a strange expression on Slade's face.

"Nah, you go over if you want. I'll probably just go back to the trailer and catch up on some sleep."

"After we both slept all damn day?" Mustang sputtered.

Slade didn't answer, he just shrugged and looked anywhere except at Mustang.

Wasn't that interesting?

Deciding to test out his newest theory, that Slade was interested in Jenna for more than just a one-night stand, Mustang casually let the bar idea go. "You're right though. Every cowboy and his brother will be at the place across the street from the arena tonight. Hey. I know what we can do."

Slade looked up. "What?"

Mustang couldn't control the wide grin he felt spreading across his face. "Maybe we can check out the bar in Jenna's hotel."

Slade's face clearly spoke his feelings about that idea. "No."

"Why not?"

"Because she didn't invite us to go snooping around her hotel."

"We wouldn't be snooping. We promised we would help her with the book. She has to fix all those facts she messed up. All that stuff you corrected. We really haven't discussed her book with her that much." *Because we were all too busy having sex to work on any book.* "So, you see, we'd be doing her a favor."

"Yeah, and I am sure that is the only reason you want to go to her hotel. To work on her book." Slade scowled. "Besides, if she wanted us there in her hotel, she wouldn't have asked us to drop her off a block away this morning so no one would see her getting out of my car."

"Oh, come on. You can't judge by that. No woman wants to get caught doing the walk of shame the morning after the night she never made it home. Being seen getting out of a car with two cowboys in it would have made it all worse."

Slade's scowl told Mustang he didn't like the walk-of-shame reference in regards to Jenna. Again, *very* interesting. "So, anyway, I'm going over to the hotel. If you want to go back to the trailer, that's fine. I'll give her your best."

That got the desired reaction from Slade.

"I didn't say I wasn't coming, just that I don't think it's a good idea. I doubt she wants us there."

Mustang grinned. Oh, she wanted them all right, and the feeling was mutual. He pushed his chair back from the table with a loud scrape. "Come on. Let's go."

Slade drew in a deep breath and then finally followed Mustang out the door.

They parked Slade's car in the lot of the hotel for the first time, having always pulled up and let Jenna out before. The two walked into the lobby and looked around.

Mustang let out a long, low whistle. "Damn, this place is nice."

It was also packed full to bursting with women of all colors, shapes and sizes, and Mustang once again felt keenly what they were missing by staying in his trailer most of the time and not in a nice hotel.

Slade's mouth twisted. "I guess it's all right. Come on. Let's just find the bar."

Mustang frowned. "Wait. Don't you want to try and find Jenna first?"

"How the hell do you propose we do that?"

"Well, first we could ask and find out if there is something happening for her conference. You know, like a dinner or something."

Slade glanced around them. "I'm thinking, judging by the thousand or so women wearing nametags and roaming the hotel lobby, that there isn't anything happening or they'd all be there."

Mustang took note of the identical nametags hanging from each and every neck. He hadn't noticed those before. He must have been looking elsewhere, like at all the exposed cleavage. "Okay, then we find a house phone and ask the front desk to call up to her room. We'll see if she's there. If not, good chance she's roaming around herself. And look, there's a bar right there in the middle of the lobby."

Slade sighed, glancing to where a group of conference attendees congregated waiting for drinks. "Okay. You go find the phone. I doubt we'll find a seat, but I'll go get us a couple of beers."

"Good deal." Mustang grinned. Anytime Slade sprung for the drinks was fine with him.

Four beers each and a few hours later, and Mustang was starting to doubt his plan. The crowds of women had thinned and dispersed, probably to their bedrooms to sleep, but not before he and Slade had gotten quite a few interested glances. However, there was still no Jenna. "I'm gonna go try to call her room again."

"Let's just go." Slade scowled, planting his empty beer bottle on the bar with a clunk.

"One more call. If she doesn't answer, we go. Okay?"

"All right. I gotta piss anyway." Slade slid off the stool they'd finally procured when the crowd had left.

"Fine, there's a house phone right next to the bathroom."

They crossed the expansive lobby, Slade disappeared into the lush marble men's room and Mustang dialed the operator once again.

"Jenna Block's room, please." Tapping the toe of his boot impatiently, Mustang listened as Jenna's phone rang and rang, but she didn't answer.

Slade emerged from the bathroom and saw him still on the phone. "Come on. Let's go. She's not there."

With a sigh, Mustang was about to give up when he turned and saw a sight that made him break out into a huge smile. "No, you're right. She's not in her room because she's right there."

Slade followed Mustang's gaze. "Holy crap. She looks like she's trashed."

"Yeah, she does." Mustang grinned and weighed the possibilities of that.

"Mustang..." Slade's voice came out as a low growl. "We're not going to take advantage of her while she's drunk."

Jenna still had yet to notice them even though she was heading straight for them, or rather for the bank of elevators just to their left.

"Slade, if we hadn't both already fu—slept with her, I might agree with you. But as it stands, we have, and I for one intend to do it again." He watched as she pushed the button for the elevator and then glanced around the lobby.

He saw the moment Jenna spotted them. Mustang was done arguing with Slade as he watched her face light up.

"You two are here?" Her voice held that high pitch that came with drinking a few too many.

Mustang smiled. "Yes we are, darlin'. Waiting on you."

He watched her melt at that. "You were waiting for me? You are both so sweet."

Next to him, Slade scowled. "Yeah, that's us. Just a couple of sweethearts."

The elevator door opened. Thankfully it was empty so Jenna wouldn't run into anyone she knew going upstairs with two cowboys. Before there could be any discussion or negotiation about who was going upstairs, Mustang took a step forward and steered Jenna inside by the elbow. He shot Slade a look. Slade finally stepped in after them and the doors glided closed.

"I can't believe you're here," Jenna announced again. That was another sign of a few too many, repeatedly noting the obvious and showing great amazement at it.

"I thought... I was afraid you were out with another woman." Jenna's eyes dropped before she finally looked up at them again.

She was jealous. That was all Mustang needed to know. He stepped into her and laid claim to her mouth with a hot, wet kiss, which she returned willingly.

An amused smile curved Mustang's lips. "Is that beer I taste, darlin'?"

Jenna looked embarrassed. "I guess. Either that or the shots."

"You were doing shots?" Slade sputtered from his place behind Jenna where he leaned unhappily against the elevator's brass railing.

Jenna turned to him. "Yeah, the boys kept buying them for us."

"The boys?" Slade lifted one shocked eyebrow so high it caused Mustang to laugh.

"What boys were those, darlin'?" Mustang asked, as interested as he was amused.

Mustang watched Jenna blush prettily. "Chase and a few of the other bull riders."

"Chase? Chase Reese? The kid up for Rookie of the Year?" Slade frowned.

"Yeah! That's him." She glanced over her shoulder at Slade, then spun back to Mustang. "He's probably gonna get Rookie of the Year if he makes both rides tomorrow night. You get a buckle for that, you know."

"You are so precious." Mustang grabbed her face and planted another kiss on her lips. "And yeah, I know about the rookie buckle. I'll even let you undo mine when we get to your room, if you want."

Mustang pulled Jenna out as the elevator doors opened, then eyed Slade who still stood inside pouting. "You coming?"

"Yeah, I'm coming." With a pissed-off look on his face, Slade finally moved before the elevator doors closed on him and he was forced to take a ride back down to the lobby.

Still amused at Slade's reaction to a little competition from the rookie, Mustang turned to Jenna. "Which way to your room, darlin'?"

She thought for a second before taking a tentative, slightly inebriated step in the direction of the hallway to their right.

Slade watched her stumble with a scowl. "Chase Reese."

Mustang laughed out loud. "Yeah, but who's she taking back to her room? Not Chase, that's for damn sure."

Slade's mouth remained screwed up in an unhappy expression. "I hope she's got a king-sized bed in there."

Mustang couldn't agree more. What he had in mind for the three of them required lots of surface area. He hung back and let Jenna get a little bit ahead of them as she led the way to her room. "I see you're done fighting with me on whether we should 'take advantage of her'."

"Yeah, I'm done. Chase frigging Reese." Slade shook his head.

Mustang laughed again. Nothing like some good old-fashioned jealousy to make a man see clearly. "Yeah, I know. The kid's got balls. I'll give him that. I guess we better show her what real men can do for her, huh?"

"Oh, yeah." Slade let out a snort. "You get a buckle for that, you know.' Yeah. I bet he made sure she knew that."

With a laugh too loud for a hotel hallway at midnight, Mustang slapped Slade on the back as they both watched Jenna in front of a door, struggling with her key card and grumbling. "Come on. Looks like she needs help getting the door open."

Then they could help her out of her clothes and help throw any memories of Chase and any possibilities regarding his buckle right out of her head.

Chapter Fifteen

"I know you think I'm drunk," Jenna announced, right after she fell over and landed on the bed while trying to get her shoes off.

Mustang laughed. "Don't worry, darlin'. We've all been there. Lucky for you, we're here to take care of you."

Slade curled his lip. *Take care of her.* Yeah. That wasn't all Mustang had in mind.

Mustang pushed Jenna's hands aside and knelt to unbuckle the ankle strap on a pair of the sexiest red, high-heel sandals Slade had ever seen. Unfortunately, any enjoyment he may have gotten from seeing Jenna in them was ruined by the thought of that rookie Chase Reese enjoying the view first.

Slade crossed his arms and watched Mustang fling one shoe into the corner of the room and move to free the other foot as Jenna continued to protest. "No, really. I'm not drunk."

Slade let out a snort. At least he knew she didn't have a car here so she hadn't driven in this condition.

"All right, darlin'. You're not drunk. Now scoot forward so I can get your dress off."

She did as Mustang instructed, sliding to the edge of the bed as he wrapped his arms around her to unzip her incredibly tantalizing red dress.

Jenna peered over Mustang's shoulder and her sleepy-looking eyes met Slade's. "Why is Slade standing all the way over there?"

Mustang turned to glance at him before he went back to wiggling the tight fabric up and over Jenna's shapely hips as she held onto his shoulders for support. "Because he thinks he's being a gentleman by staying all the way over there."

Slade scowled at that as Jenna frowned at Mustang. "What?"

"He thinks you're too drunk and we're taking advantage of you, darlin'."

Just like Chase probably would have taken advantage of her if she'd stayed at the bar any longer. Slade shot a less-than-friendly look at Mustang. "I don't *think* she's too drunk. I know."

"I told you, I'm not." With that, she let out an incredibly adorable beer-and-shot-fueled burp. Eyes opening wide, Jenna's hand flew up to cover her mouth. "Oops. Sorry. Maybe I am a little bit drunk."

Slade raised his brow. "You think?"

Her eyes narrowed at him. "That doesn't mean I can't make a rational decision."

Slade glowered. "That's exactly what it means."

"No. I was sober all day long and all I could think about was having sex with you two again. That's why I went to the bar in the first place. To find you."

Mustang's face broke out into an amused grin. "So there you go, Slade. She made the decision before she got drunk."

"Exactly." Jenna nodded her head so hard in agreement with Mustang that she lost her balance and barely caught herself before she fell over sideways on the bed.

Slade shook his head and sighed. She looked so damned tempting, perched on the edge of the bed in nothing but lacy undies and bra. It should have been easy to just let himself sink into her. Any other time, with any other woman and he would have.

Why did the fact this was Jenna and not just some random, nameless woman make him change his rules? He was afraid to answer that question.

Jenna reached one wobbly arm out toward him. "Come here."

Against his better judgment, Slade did just that, letting her grab his hand and pull him closer.

"Kiss me."

Slade glanced at Mustang, who had finished undressing Jenna and was now seated in the chair just off to the side of the bed.

"Better do as the lady says, Slade." Mustang pulled off one boot and let it drop to the floor.

Looking down at Jenna and seeing the need in her face, Slade gave up the fight.

He glanced at Mustang again. "You come prepared?"

Mustang snorted. "Of course, I did. Who do you think you're talking to?"

Dragging in a steadying breath, Slade gave in. He pushed Jenna back onto the bed, climbed on top of her mostly naked body and did as she asked, kissing her with all he had, knowing he'd lost not just the battle, but also the war.

Slade finally opened his eyes, coming back to reality again when the mattress dipped and Mustang crawled onto the bed. Mustang placed both a tube of lubricant and a strip of condoms on the spread next to him.

Swallowing hard, Slade glanced at Mustang, suspecting what his friend had in mind for Jenna judging by the items lying so innocently on the bed. The thought had Slade so excited he could feel his rapid heartbeat all the way down into his erection.

Slade looked again to Mustang. "You sure she's ready for this?"

Mustang nodded. "I think so, and if she's not, she'll let us know. She's a big girl, Slade."

Meanwhile, Jenna was struggling to get Slade's jeans off, proving Mustang's point that ready or not, she was at least willing.

After the slightest hesitation, Slade stood and quickly undid the buttons of his shirt. His belt and the fly on his jeans soon followed. Slade sat in the same chair Mustang had occupied and watched Mustang crawl farther up the bed.

Slade's eyes never left the bed as, with a grin, Mustang rolled on top of Jenna and slid one hand between her legs. Bending both knees, Jenna spread her legs further apart for Mustang. Slade swallowed the acid in his throat as Jenna raised her hips off the bed and groaned while Mustang stroked her.

Yanking his boots off in record time, Slade dumped them on the floor, stripped off the rest of his clothes and made his way to the bed just in time to see Jenna start to shake. With one hand behind her head, Slade clamped his mouth over hers and kissed her for all he was worth. It may be Mustang making her come, but she was kissing Slade while she did.

Her tremors subsided and Mustang shifted on the bed. "Roll on up there on top of Slade, darlin'."

Slade lay on his back as Jenna rolled boneless on top of him, straddling him as Mustang had asked.

Jenna braced on her arms and leaned down to kiss Slade again, which was fine with him, except that it also thrust her beautiful ass right up in front of Mustang. Knowing Mustang, he was going to take full advantage of that fact.

Slade's heart beat faster as Mustang reached between Jenna's thighs again with one hand while struggling to blindly find the condoms and lube with his other.

As Mustang kneeled on the bed behind Jenna, his hand finally connected with the tube and he grinned. Mustang's hand withdrew from Jenna as he opened the cap.

Slade tried to ignore the slight tremble of his hands as he tangled them in Jenna's hair and held her head to kiss her deeper. He closed his eyes, knowing what Mustang was going to do, and not wanting to see it.

He felt her body still, heard her breath catch in her throat and pictured Mustang's cold, slick finger pressing against her anus. The slightest pressure would have the tip of the digit slipping inside her. Slade felt Jenna tense above him, felt every muscle in her brace and tighten, and heard her take in a sharp breath.

"You all right, darlin'?" Mustang asked from behind her.

Jenna nodded but still held her body stiffly above Slade.

Slade grabbed Jenna's face and made her look at him. "Are you sure, Jenna?"

"Yes." She drew in another quick breath. "I'm okay."

Mustang reached around the front of Jenna with his other hand and connected with her clit. "Just relax, darlin', and let old Mustang take care of you."

Jenna's eyes practically rolled back in her head and she started to moan from whatever Mustang was doing to her between her thighs. Slade felt the tension leave Jenna's muscles. The more Mustang worked, the more she relaxed until her chest was lying flat on Slade's, her ass still in the air for Mustang's taking.

Looking past Jenna's body as she writhed on top of him, Slade watched Mustang slide in a second finger. Jenna's torso bowed, pushing her against his hand and forcing the two digits deeper inside her while he worked her clit.

Slade swallowed hard as he felt her body begin to tremble. She was close to coming again from Mustang's attentions and once again, Slade wasn't involved in it.

He saw Mustang squeeze more lube and spread the stuff on his condom-covered erection as best he could one-handed. Mustang withdrew his fingers and replaced them with the head of his cock, pressing slowly against Jenna. Slade had never felt so jealous in all his life.

Slade knew exactly what was to come. He'd been party to it enough times. As Jenna started to come, Mustang would push inside her before she had time to get nervous and tense up.

Jenna gasped as the wide head breached her tight ring of muscle. He braced a hand on each of her gorgeous hips as Mustang pushed deeper, past the resistance. Once there, Mustang held himself motionless.

Slade felt Jenna breathing heavily above him as she adjusted to the sensations he suspected she wasn't used to.

"You okay?" Slade asked.

She held perfectly still and breathed deeply. Eyes squeezed tight, she nodded.

"Have you done this before?"

Opening her eyes, Jenna let out a breathy laugh, suddenly sounding pretty near sober. "Which? The anal? Or two men at once?"

As Mustang held himself pressed deep inside her, ready to pounce, Slade kissed her trembling mouth. "Both, I guess."

"Yes to the first, no to the second." Then she laughed again. "But never with anyone as big as Mustang."

Mustang chuckled at that, though his face showed the strain of staying still inside her. "It'll be fine, darlin'. I promise. Just relax."

"We don't have to do this if it hurts you. Mustang can pull out." Slade liked that idea more than he could say. What he would have given to be alone with Jenna tonight, or even to just swap positions with Mustang so he could be the one taking her instead.

Mustang leaned over her back, moving her hair as he kissed up and down her neck. One hand moved to thumb her nipple while the other began moving on her clit again. "You're okay? Right, darlin'?"

Jenna nodded, trembling slightly beneath his hands.

Tired of being left out of the party, Slade reached over, grabbed a condom and ripped open the foil.

He felt Jenna draw in a sharp breath at the sight. "Think you can handle Slade too, darlin'? If not, we can come up with alternate arrangements. It's up to you."

She slowly straightened upright and had Mustang drawing in a breath of his own. Slade could only imagine what her body was doing to Mustang as she squeezed him in new and wonderful ways. Slade waited, unmoving, impatient for her answer before he entered her.

"No, really, it's okay. I want this. I want to feel both of you inside me. I've been thinking about it a lot the last few days." Jenna sounded totally lucid now.

That was all Slade needed to hear.

Slade watched the hand Mustang had wrapped around Jenna roam up from her clit to her belly. She was so beautiful, even with another man's hands on her.

Jenna's body jerked when Mustang's tongue made contact with her ear, and Slade took the chance to move, sliding inside her.

Feeling himself beginning to slip out as she tensed up, Slade held her hips and pushed a little deeper. He felt her breath quicken.

Slade managed to detach his brain for a moment and just feel what it was like to love Jenna for a few brief, blissful moments, until Mustang positioned himself to begin moving as well.

Holding himself motionless, Slade grit his teeth, bracing for what he knew was coming. The already tight quarters inside Jenna were even more crowded with both of them contained there.

Mustang started to move slowly, and every stroke rubbed against Slade. Separated by only a thin wall, Slade felt Mustang's cock rub against his inside Jenna and he remembered exactly why they rarely did this. It was a little too close for comfort.

Slade reached his hand between Jenna's legs, about to try and make her come, when he realized Mustang's balls were pretty much right there. He pulled his hand back and left it on Jenna's waist instead. "Make her come, Mustang. Please. I need to feel something besides you in there."

Mustang chuckled and slid a hand around and down to find Jenna's swollen clit.

Slade closed his eyes and moved in a rhythm opposite of Mustang's, deciding things were better if he was pulled out while Mustang was in, but once Jenna bent low over Slade's chest and he felt the orgasm start to rock her body, none of the rest mattered. He held on tightly and enjoyed the ride, finishing himself with one hell of a body-rocking climax.

He shuddered and then pulled out gently, sad to leave her warmth, but staying inside after he'd come and feeling Mustang rub against him was just too much.

Slade was even sadder when he realized what Mustang had in mind now that Slade had backed off. He watched Mustang pull out and adjust Jenna's position, flipping her over onto her back so she lay on the bed. Mustang pushed her knees up to her chest, his length poised again at the entrance he'd just vacated. "I like watching your face, darlin'."

Jenna's throat worked, swallowing hard as Mustang pushed back inside.

"You feel so damn good. I need to move more. I wanna fuck you fast and hard. Ah, Jenna. Please? Can I?"

Jenna took in a deep shaky breath. "Can we use some more lube first?"

Mustang laughed. "Sure thing, darlin'."

With more than a bit of jealousy, Slade watched Mustang pull out and use his fingers to spread more lubricant. Then he pushed inside her ass again, disappearing slowly inside as she took him in.

Slade heard Jenna's intake of breath as Mustang slid deeply inside her. He saw the look of pure ecstasy on Mustang's face as, inch by inch, Jenna's body engulfed him completely. Then Mustang's apparently talented fingers slid between her thighs. In moments, he had Jenna loudly coming again as he fucked her—and yes, that was the only word to describe what Mustang was doing to Jenna in that big bed as Slade looked on.

Why the hell didn't Mustang just finish already? Even better, why couldn't he have just come when Slade had?

Not sure which was worse, watching them together or knowing it was happening while not watching, Slade finally decided to go to the bathroom to clean up. But even the rushing of the running water in the sink didn't cover the sound of when his best friend came inside of the woman Slade wanted all for himself, and that really sucked.

Chapter Sixteen

Mustang stretched his arms above his head and twisted slowly, hoping to work the kinks of a night of kinky sex with Jenna out of his muscles before he rode. He didn't always warm up as much as he should before a ride, especially when he was too busy checking out the scenery. But tonight, particularly since this was the championship round and it was guaranteed they'd be facing the rankest bulls on the circuit, Mustang made sure to stretch.

He bent to one side and caught a glimpse of Slade's scowl. "What the hell is wrong with you?"

"You."

"Me? What did I do?" Now that he thought about it, Mustang realized Slade had been oddly quiet and crankier than usual ever since they'd rolled out of Jenna's king-sized bed early that morning.

"Nothing, forget about it," Slade grumbled.

"No, I won't forget about it. If you're pissed, tell me why." Any and every ride could be their last and Mustang wasn't about to get on the back of two thousand pounds of bucking bull knowing that his best friend wasn't talking to him.

"Fine. Did you have to...you know...do that with Jenna last night?"

Mustang frowned. "No, I don't know. Do what? What are you talking about?"

As a couple of other riders walked past, Slade lowered his voice so much, Mustang had to lean closer to hear him. "Did you have to take her like that? You know. There. And so rough? Maybe she didn't want to do that."

What? Mustang didn't get to do what he'd done with Jenna last night as often as he'd like, but he still had done it before, and with Slade right there along for the ride, so what was his problem now?

He suspected this had nothing to do with what Mustang had done with Jenna, and everything to do with how Slade felt about it.

This was all bullshit and Mustang knew it. Slade had never cared in the past when he slid in anywhere, whether it was right after him, or before him, or at the same time for that matter.

Mustang could see the real problem was that Slade was falling for Jenna, but he had a feeling not even a charging bull could get Slade to admit that.

"Slade, I asked her first and she said okay. What more did you want me to do? Besides that, judging by how hard she came from it, she liked it just fine. The harder and faster the better, apparently." Mustang had lowered his voice to what he thought was an appropriately discreet volume, but Slade still glanced around them.

"Shh!" Slade looked like he was resisting the urge to punch Mustang as he set his jaw. "Stop saying shit like that about her."

Mustang laughed, which turned Slade's face a lovely shade of angry red. Oh, yeah. Slade was falling hard and fast, and Mustang had every intention of torturing him on the way down.

"Okay. Then what do you want me to say?" Mustang lowered his voice again and decided to push Slade a little further, just for fun. "Maybe you want me to start talking in code now. Here, how's this? Since she said she'd already had her virgin rosebud deflowered before we got to her, I figured it was okay if I fully enjoyed a taste of her forbidden fruit. There. Was that better? But wait, I'm mixing my, what are they called? Metaphors. That's it. Would that particular part of Jenna's anatomy be referred to as a fruit or a flower, do you think?"

The look on Slade's face at that question made Mustang glad he used to sneak a peek into his mother's romance novels back when he was a kid so he could be so creative in his torture.

"You can be such an ass. That shit is no better so just shut the hell up about the whole thing." Slade scowled.

Mustang grinned. "Yeah, I didn't think you'd like that either. Now, you better get over yourself because I left a ticket for Jenna at the box office. She promised she's going to be here tonight and I intend on taking full advantage of what is most likely our last night with her. Got it?"

If Mustang's theory was correct and Slade had it bad for Jenna, things were only going to go downhill for their happy little threesome. If he thought Slade was cranky now, Mustang could just imagine how unbearable he was going to be when Jenna left for New York and they both went home for the off-season.

It was going to be one hell of a long, horrible drive back home to Texas with a pissy Slade riding shotgun in the passenger seat.

Chase Reese walked by with his usual schoolboy smile and friendly greeting for them both, and Mustang watched Slade's face turn even stonier than it had been before. In fact, he even thought he heard a low growl rumbling in Slade's chest.

Mustang grinned. The poor kid had no idea what he'd done. By simply buying a few shots for a pretty woman at a bar he'd probably made an enemy for life. Yup, Slade had it bad, and if it didn't make him so damn cranky, Mustang would really enjoy watching the mighty one fall. But right now, Mustang had a bull ride to worry about. "I'm going on out."

"Fine."

"You coming?"

"No."

All righty, then. Mustang left his crabby friend licking his wounds in the locker room and headed out to behind the chutes, keeping half an eye out for Jenna in the stands.

He kept looking for her in the VIP box, but by the time the rides started, she still hadn't appeared, and Mustang had to wonder if maybe Slade wasn't crazy. What if they had pushed her too far last night and she was avoiding them?

After having spent an entire season working to avoid the day-after confrontation with his and Slade's conquests at all costs, the irony of Jenna dodging them was definitely not lost on Mustang.

Mustang took one more wistful look at the empty seat in the VIP box and then went to get his bull rope.

Chapter Seventeen

"Hey, there. When did you sneak in here?" Chase swung up on the railing in front of Jenna's seat, grinning wide.

Jenna groaned. "I know, I'm really late. I had a dinner I couldn't miss. I got here as soon as I could."

"Your friends aren't with you? The guys will be very disappointed."

Jenna laughed. "I'm sure they will be. But sorry, I didn't tell them I was coming."

"The secret book?" Chase lowered his voice conspiratorially.

"Yeah."

Something happening in the center of the arena caught Jenna's attention. Chase followed her gaze then looked back to her. "What's got you frowning like that, beautiful?"

Jenna hadn't realized she had been frowning. She'd have to try and remember to stop doing that before she got wrinkles.

"What's happening out there?" Jenna nodded in the direction of the line of riders forming in the middle of the arena. "Is this like an awards ceremony?"

Chase laughed. "No. It's the draft. The top fifteen riders get to pick which bulls they want to ride for the short-go in the championship round. I can't stay here too long, I gotta go get on that line myself. I just wanted to say hello."

She spotted Slade at the head of the line. Saying hello was more than Slade had bothered to do. Even if she had arrived late, you'd still think he and Mustang would have at least waved at her or something. They must have noticed her eventual arrival. Chase had.

Smothering a pout at that, Jenna mustered a smile for Chase. "Thanks. That's sweet of you. But I thought you guys were assigned what bulls you rode."

"That's called the draw, but that's for the long round. For the short round, the top riders get to choose."

Hmm. Made sense. Kind of. "So you'd want to choose the easiest bull so you don't fall off, right?"

Chase looked at her like she'd grown another head. "Heck no. You try and pick the rankest bull so you'll get a higher score. The judges don't give points for easy."

"Ah." This sport was way more complicated than she'd first thought. In fact, she'd probably done the stupidest thing ever by making her hero a bull rider, not that her cowboy book would ever see the light of day.

Jenna felt her brow furrow again at that thought and resisted the urge to physically smooth the wrinkles away with one hand. Instead, she looked up at Chase when she remembered he had to ride two bulls tonight to win Rookie of the Year. "Did you already ride?"

His face nearly glowed as he answered. "Yes, ma'am. I got an eighty-nine."

She smiled, pretending like she knew what that number meant. "Good for you. You have to ride one more to get that buckle, right?"

Chase grinned wide. "Yup. Just got to ride one in the short-go."

"But wait...then you don't want to pick a hard bull in the draw, I mean draft. Wouldn't you want to pick an easy bull so you have a better chance of staying on?"

Chase rolled his eyes. "*No* bulls in the short-go of the championships are easy, Jenna. These are the rankest bulls on the circuit. Some of them are up for Bull of the Year."

Bull of the Year? Jenna smothered a laugh at that revelation. Then she stifled the fear that the more she learned the more she realized she didn't know.

"Just be careful, okay? Don't choose one that's too rank." And if that wasn't the most god-awful word she'd ever heard, she didn't know what was, but her use of it earned her a smile from Chase.

"I won't, Jenna. Promise. Besides, the top guys get to choose first and they'll get the rankest bulls before I even get up there." He glanced at the center of the arena. "I'm gonna have to go but you know what would make me ride a whole lot better?"

Suspicious, Jenna asked doubtfully, "No. What would that be?"

"A kiss from the prettiest girl here."

How could a guy look so innocent and yet so sinful at the same time? But given how sweetly he'd asked, how could she say no?

Besides, the way Slade and Mustang were ignoring her, they weren't acting like they cared what she did or with whom, even after all they'd done together the night before. Her cheeks heated at the memory of Slade beneath her, sliding in while Mustang was behind, buried deep inside her...

Jenna shook that memory away. "Okay, but just a quick one. On the cheek," she added quickly.

"Sounds good." Chase bent closer as Jenna leaned forward, but her aim was off and not helped by Chase turning his head to ensure it would be. The kiss landed smack on his lips.

Jenna's face felt on fire. She peered around to see who'd noticed as Chase jumped down to the ground, grinning. "Now, I'll definitely win Rookie of the Year."

"Glad I could help." She couldn't help but smile. Rolling her eyes, she sent him off to pick his bull.

$$*$$

As the first-place-ranked rider bantered with the announcer and discussed which bull he'd be choosing for the short round, Slade made the huge mistake of letting his gaze stray to the stands and scowled at what he saw. "Jenna's here."

Mustang, in line two riders behind Slade, spun to look. "I've been checking for her all night and she wasn't there."

"She's here now."

Mustang squinted at the stands. "Where is she?"

Slade snorted out a bitter laugh. "Right behind Chase Reese, that's where."

"What?" Mustang must have finally spotted her too, just as Chase leaned in and kissed her. "I'll be damned. Look at that. This kid doesn't give up, does he?"

"The way she's encouraging him, why should he give up?" Slade guessed Chase would be the one in Jenna's big bed that night. At that thought, he wondered angrily if the maid had changed Jenna's lube-stained sheets or if Chase would have to wallow in them dirty.

Chase, apparently done kissing Jenna, ran to the center of the arena and took his place near the back of the line just as it was Slade's turn to step up onto the announcer's platform and pick his bull.

"Slade Bower. You came into this competition ranked number three in the world. You're going into the championship round of the season finals in the number-two position. Given how tight the standings are, the number-one position is up for grabs and within reach for you. You have experience with some of the bulls in this draft. Which one will you choose tonight?"

A microphone was thrust in front of his face as the announcer angled the list of fifteen bulls toward Slade, not that he needed to see it. Only one bull had been crossed off the list as yet, the bull the number-one rider had chosen.

Slade had studied the list back in the locker room, and had made a decision there, but he didn't say the name he'd circled on his own list. Instead, he heard himself say, "I'll take Ballbreaker."

"Ballbreaker. That's a bold choice, Slade. That bull is unridden after eighteen times out. He bucked off the number-one rider the first night of this series."

"Yes, sir."

The announcer laughed. "Okay, then. Slade Bower takes Ballbreaker."

Slade tipped his hat, turned and walked back down the steps, noticing the surprised look on Mustang's face.

"Are you nuts?" Mustang asked as Slade passed.

He paused, mid-step. "Sorry, did you want him?"

Mustang frowned. "Hell no." Then Mustang was called up to the platform and the announcer's banter for the crowd continued.

His choice made, Slade had nothing left to do now but wait for the remaining riders to choose. Oh, yeah, and he had to ride Ballbreaker to the buzzer. *Piece of cake.*

Slade walked past the riders at the end of the line, including Chase. He paused at what he saw. "You've got lipstick on your face."

The rookie didn't even have the sense to look ashamed. Instead, Chase wiped his mouth with the back of his hand and grinned. "Thanks."

Slade grunted his response to the kid's thanks, but he was pretty sure what came out sounded more like a growl.

Chapter Eighteen

"Do you know what you're doing?"

Slade frowned at Mustang. "What are you talking about?"

"Ballbreaker. What the hell, Slade? What about One-Night Stand? He was in the draft for the short round, you've already ridden him, and you got a ninety point score on him."

Some days there was just no making Mustang happy. Slade sighed. "Yeah, well, you should be happy, because I didn't pick him in the draft, you could. So now you have him and you can get the high score."

Mustang shook his head. "I don't know what you're out to prove."

The announcer's voice captured Slade's attention. "Chase Reese, up for Rookie of the Year, aboard Good Night Ladies."

Slade frowned, all of his concentration focused on the rookie climbing onto the rails of the bucking chute. "I'm not out to prove nothing. Now shut up. I'm trying to watch."

Mustang followed the direction of Slade's gaze. "This is about Chase? Are you freaking crazy?"

Far more interested in watching the bastard who had been kissing Jenna ride, Slade didn't answer, but instead jumped up on the rail to get a better look.

Finally, thankfully, off the topic of Slade's choice of bulls for a second, Mustang climbed up next to him as the gate opened and bull and rider took off. "Chase better dress that ride up a bit if he wants anything higher than an eighty the way that bull is bucking tonight."

"Maybe he should have chosen a better bull." Slade raised a brow and shot a look at Mustang.

Mustang snorted. "You mean like Ballbreaker?"

Slade shrugged.

"The score doesn't matter anyway. If he covers the ride, he wins the rookie buckle," Mustang pointed out.

Focused on the action in the arena, Slade tuned out Mustang as the bull continued to spin into Chase's hand.

Getting into the kid's ride, Mustang started a running commentary next to Slade. He started out soft enough but ended up shouting, annoying Slade even more.

"The bull's slowing down. Spur him, Chase! Yeah, that's it." Mustang slapped Slade in the arm. "Chase looks great. The kid's doing everything right."

"Yeah, whatever." Slade's competitive side kicked in as Chase maintained textbook form, spurring the bull with his outside leg to keep him rounding to the right, intentionally showing a little daylight between his leg and the bull to dress up the ride. The rookie looked perfect, right until the buzzer when he jumped down, landing on his feet with a grin.

Yup, Chase was the kind who always landed on his feet. Slade hated that.

"Eighty-eight point five!" the arena announcer told the crowd.

"Ooo wee! That's a good score."

"Yeah," Slade grumbled. "Considering it was the easiest bull in the draft." And the damn kid didn't even have to get dirty to earn it.

"No bulls in the short round are easy. You know that. Good Night Ladies was just having a bad night, but Chase pulled it off. You have to hand it to him."

Slade turned away from the arena while Mustang kept rambling about Chase. Slade ignored him mostly until Mustang raised an arm and waved. "Hey, Slade. Jenna's waving at us."

Jenna. Great. She was probably waving at Chase. "Yeah. So?"

"Since we don't have time to say hello to her before we ride, it might be nice if you waved back." Mustang frowned at him.

Slade climbed down from the rail, pointedly not looking in Jenna's direction. "I'm going to stretch."

Mustang climbed down next to him, shaking his head. "I seriously hope that Ballbreaker bucks this bad mood out of you."

As Slade spotted Chase running over to Jenna's seat in the stands and saw her jump up to hug him, he decided even Ballbreaker wasn't up to that monumental task.

The short round in the finals always went fast. Being the top fifteen riders, riding the top bulls of the season, there was no messing around in the chutes. Everyone, man and beast, just jumped in and got right down to business.

In what felt like mere minutes, the thirteen other riders, including Mustang, had ridden, and it was Slade's turn in the chute.

"Well folks, Slade Bower started out the season wearing a number nine on his back after placing ninth in the world last season. He's ridden his way up to begin this championship series in the number-three position for the season and the number-two spot this championship, and if he can get a qualified ride in the short round tonight, it could earn him a number one on his vest when we come back next year. But standing in his way is Ballbreaker. Unridden after eighteen times out, this bull bested Slade's good friend, Mustang Jackson, in Kansas City last week."

Slade worked to tune out his surroundings, both the echoing voice of the announcer and the fact that Jenna, whose lipstick had been smeared all over Chase Reese's mouth, was seated not far from him, directly behind the chutes.

As Slade climbed up onto the rails of the bucking chute, Mustang was right there next to him.

Still wearing his dust-covered vest from jumping off One-Night Stand at the buzzer after a successful ride, Mustang continued reviewing everything he'd already battered into Slade's brain since the moment Slade had picked Ballbreaker in the draft. "Remember, this bull keeps changing it up. He'll go right first, but then he'll reverse and go left, then he bucks straight out. That's what you have to worry about. The way he snaps his back—"

Slade nodded. "Okay, Mustang, I got it. I heard you the first two times you told me."

Head down, Slade pulled his rope and wrapped it tightly around his glove. He pushed his hat lower onto his head with his free hand, clamped his legs against the bull's sides and nodded. The gate swung open and away they went.

Heels in, toes out, Slade braced for Ballbreaker's first reversal. Bearing down, he stayed on through the bull's powerful snaps and twists. As the eight seconds stretched out to feel more like eight minutes, Slade made one correction to his position after another. He finally heard the buzzer just as Ballbreaker snapped his butt so hard into the air that he flipped Slade up and over his horns.

Caught up in his rope good and tight, Slade dangled like a rag doll by one hand. He was aware of the bullfighters moving in as he tried to free his hand from the rope. He knew he had to stay on his feet even while Ballbreaker continued to buck and spin, dragging Slade with him.

He felt hands trying to free him from the rope as Ballbreaker hopped, throwing Slade into the air and off his feet. When he landed in the dirt on his ass, Slade saw hooves and horns coming at him.

He turned his head and, for the first time in a long time, prayed.

Everything happened in a blur. It seemed that one moment his arm was being pulled out of its socket, then the next he was lying in the dirt flat on his back, staring up at the glare of the arena lights with no idea how he'd gotten in that position. Slade felt something warm trickling into his eye and then gauze was pressed against his head.

The sports-medicine team surrounded him, asking questions, but it was beyond Slade to answer them at the moment.

"Can you tell me where it hurts?"

Where doesn't it hurt? Slade started to chuckle, then he realized it hurt too much to do that.

When he didn't answer the doctor asked again, and this time Slade answered. "Everywhere."

At that vague answer, the doctor switched tactics and got more specific. "Can you move your feet?"

God! Do they think I'm paralyzed? Horrified at that thought, Slade concentrated and moved first one leg, bending it at the knee, then the other. "Yeah."

"Okay. Good. Does your neck hurt?"

Unridden

Slade slowly shook his head no, which made his head feel like a screwdriver was being jammed behind his eyes, but at least his neck didn't hurt...not too much, anyway.

That small movement seemed to make them all happy. The doctor moved on to quizzing Slade with thought-provoking questions now that the physical tests seemed done. Meanwhile, all Slade really wanted to do was close his eyes for just a little bit. The dirt was soft and cool and really didn't make a bad bed in a pinch. If only they'd leave him alone for a while so he could rest.

"Can you tell me your name?" Slade heard the question from somewhere off in the distance.

When he didn't answer right away, his cheek was slapped lightly. Frowning, Slade opened his eyes again. "Slade Bower."

"What city are we in?"

"Kansas... No, Tulsa." That was a hard question on a good day the way they moved around. Hoping that correct answer meant they'd finally stop with the questions, Slade was disappointed when the doctor continued.

"What bull were you on tonight, Slade?"

That one was easy. "Ballbreaker."

The doctor laughed lightly. "He was that, wasn't he?"

"Yeah." Slade let out a short laugh, realizing it was a mistake immediately when it made everything hurt. "What was my score?"

The doctor laughed again. "When they start worrying about their score, I know they're all right. We'll find that out for you in a second, Slade. Do you want to try sitting up or do you want the stretcher?"

Stubborn to the core, Slade shook his head. "No stretcher." But that meant he needed to get up, and as countless hands

161

began to pull him from the dirt, he realized his riding arm, dangling painfully, was useless. "My arm..."

"Yeah, it's dislocated. We'll get it fixed up in the back."

Great. That was always fun.

Sitting up brought to light a new pain. Slade hissed in a painful breath of air. "I think my ribs are broke."

The doctor nodded. "Yeah, I'm not surprised. You got trampled on pretty good. You may need stitches on that head wound and my bet is you've got yourself a nice concussion too."

"I guess it's a good thing I've got a few months off then, isn't it?"

The doctor grinned. "Because if this wasn't the last ride of the season you'd be on a bull again next week, wouldn't you?"

"Hell yeah." Slade let out a laugh followed by a groan. "Ow."

Shaking his head, the doctor wrapped one arm around Slade's waist, supporting him as the crowd in the arena, which Slade realized had been eerily silent up until then, erupted in cheers.

Mustang was there next to Slade as soon as they got behind the chutes. "You okay?"

"Never been better." If you didn't count the concussion, broken ribs and dislocated shoulder.

The group headed down the long, seemingly never-ending hallway to the medical room half-filled with bull riders nursing various degrees of injury.

Mustang took one look around the room. "Looks like the docs have been busy tonight."

Helping Slade up onto an available table, the doctor nodded, grinning. "I can always count on you boys to keep me busy. Good thing too. The missus has her eye on a new car. I'm going to give you some muscle relaxers, Slade, and then we'll get that shoulder popped back in."

As the doctor moved off, Mustang raised a brow at Slade. "Good ride."

Slade laughed, then held his ribs. "Yeah, until the end."

Mustang's eyes cut to the television monitor set up in the corner. "Looks like you finished in second place."

"Second?" Slade's mouth twisted into a scowl at that information.

Mustang nodded. "Yeah. Jorge did really well too. He held onto the number-one spot, even with your ninety-point-five score in the short-go."

"Ninety point five?" Slade smiled. "Told you Ballbreaker wasn't the wrong choice."

Stepping back out of the way so the doctor could tend to Slade, Mustang laughed. "We'll see if you still feel that way after the doc here snaps your shoulder back in the socket."

Slade went to shrug then realized he couldn't. "Won't be the first time."

Mustang grinned. "Nor the last, God willing."

"God willing." Slade gave a quick, silent word of thanks that he'd been blessed with walking away one more time.

Chapter Nineteen

Jenna pushed past the knees of the people in her row, tripping over someone's feet in her struggle to get down to where they had just carried Slade barely a minute before. Yeah, he'd been on his feet when they'd taken him out, but only because of the two men supporting him on either side. He'd been clutching one arm while blood soaked through the cloth a third man held against Slade's head.

Tears blurring her eyes and her heart pounding so loudly it drowned out the noise of the crowd, Jenna ran head on into Chase.

He grabbed both of her arms. "Jenna. What's wrong?"

"What's wrong?" Hadn't Chase seen Slade getting dragged around underneath the bull? Hadn't he seen him lying there motionless after the animal pounced on him? "I have to get to Slade."

"He's in with the sports-medicine team." Chase didn't release her arms, but held her even as she struggled to push past him to go find Slade. Then Chase's eyes opened wide as he stared at her face. "Oh my God. You're with Slade?"

Not worrying about the details, Jenna managed to nod. She could see as all the pieces started to fall together in Chase's brain.

"That's why you're in the VIP seats. That's why you said at the bar you weren't really available."

Chase dropped his grip on her arms and ran one hand over his face.

"Holy crap! I kissed you. Shit! I kissed Slade Bower's girl." Chase paced in a tight circle. "Jenna, why didn't you tell me?"

"Because it's more complicated than you can even imagine." Jenna let out a frustrated breath. "Listen. Can you get me back there to him?"

"No wonder he looked so pissed during the draft after I kissed you. I'm lucky he didn't beat the crap out of me."

"Chase. Stop." Jenna debated what to say and finally blurted out, "Slade and I aren't serious so don't worry about it. Okay?"

Hmm, uttering that truth out loud hurt more than she'd anticipated.

"Slade sure as hell looked serious when he spotted your lipstick on my face during the draft."

Jenna decided Chase was too far gone in his hero worship of Slade to think clearly. Giving up on trying to make him feel better while she was too upset to think herself, she turned away. Her intention was to follow the same hall she'd seen Slade disappear down and try and find him.

She was about to start searching for him alone when a man wearing some sort of ID badge around his neck and a cowboy hat on his head stepped in front of her.

"Where do you think you're going, little lady?"

Maybe if she acted as if she belonged there, he'd let her pass. Dragging out her tough New Yorker attitude, Jenna made the announcement with as much authority as she could muster at the moment. "I'm going to see Slade Bower."

"Only family members are allowed back there. You family?"

Jenna debated which lie to use. *He's my brother* crossed her mind, but she didn't know if Slade even had a sister or if this guy would know her if he did.

"It's okay. She's his girlfriend." Chase stepped up behind her. When the man raised a brow doubtfully, Chase continued. "Didn't you see her there in the VIP seats? I'll take her back and make sure she gets where she's going, if you want."

That promise got them a nod as the man moved out of their way.

Relieved to finally be going somewhere, Jenna looked up at Chase as they made their way down a long hallway. "Thanks. I owe you."

Chase let out a laugh. "Tell Slade not to kill me for kissing you and I'll call it even."

They entered a room full of what looked like beds or examination tables. Cowboys in various states of undress lounged on a number of them.

She scanned all the faces quickly until she found Slade, pale and unmoving with his eyes closed. The shirt stained with the blood from his head wound lay crumpled in a ball on the table next to him.

Why was no one tending to him? Jenna swallowed hard, afraid. What if he had internal injuries and no one was keeping an eye on him? What if he was dead and no one had noticed yet? That thought nearly sent her careening to the floor.

She took a step closer, shaking so badly she could barely stand. Just as Jenna started to feel lightheaded and as if she might black out right there, she heard boots on the tile floor. She spun to look at the doorway as a welcome, familiar face appeared.

"Mustang." Pushing past Chase, Jenna threw herself at Mustang. All the horror of watching Slade getting trampled, of holding her breath in the deathly silent arena as she waited along with the thousands of others to find out if he was still alive, the fear now at his being unconscious, possibly dead, the way he looked so horrible... It all finally came to a head and she found herself hysterical, sobbing in Mustang's arms.

Mustang pulled her out into the hallway and she didn't protest. Once outside, he held her. "Shh. It's okay, darlin'."

Barely coherent, Jenna asked, "What's wrong with him?"

"Slade? He'll be fine."

Fine? He didn't look fine. Jenna swallowed past the lump in her throat. "He looks...dead."

Mustang smiled at her reassuringly. "He's not dead, darlin'. He's sleeping. He was snoring before when I left. There's nothing wrong with him that won't heal."

Jenna let her head fall against Mustang's chest and released a laugh of relief in the midst of her tears. "Thank God. I was so worried when I saw him under that bull."

Jenna was about to launch into more specific questions about Slade's injuries when Chase stepped forward. "Listen, Mustang. I have to apologize, man. I had no idea she was with Slade. Honestly. If I'd known Jenna was his girlfriend, I never would have gone anywhere near her. You know I respect Slade more than I can say. I look up to both of you guys."

Mustang looked down at Jenna before answering Chase. "Relax, kid. It's fine. Really."

Chase looked like a little boy who'd just been forgiven for stealing cookies from the kitchen jar. "You sure?"

"Yeah. You and I are good. Don't worry."

Hesitating, Chase glanced back at the doorway they'd just left and winced. "What about Slade? He was pretty pissed at me during the draft."

"I'll tell him what you said. He'll be fine."

Letting out a big breath, Chase appeared relieved. "Okay. Thanks, man. Um, I'm gonna go out now. They need to interview me."

"Yeah. Congratulations on Rookie of the Year, by the way."

"Thanks." Red-faced and still looking contrite, Chase glanced one last time at Jenna and then exited down the hall, which left Mustang to question Jenna.

"*So*, you're Slade's girlfriend now, huh?" Mustang ran one hand up and down her back, comforting her even as he looked amused.

Still shaky, Jenna shook her head at Mustang. "I never said that. Chase assumed it. I couldn't exactly tell him the truth, now could I?"

"No. Guess not. It's okay. I don't get my feelings hurt that easily. I'm sure if it was me there laid up in that bed instead of Slade you'd be just as upset."

Jenna was in no mood for teasing. All she wanted to do was go back in and see Slade open his eyes and prove he wasn't dead. "Of course I'd be just as upset if that was you."

"Oh, yeah, I'm sure."

"It's true!"

"I know, darlin'. I'm just teasing you." Mustang grinned as he ran his hands up her back, finally settling them on each side of her face as he lowered his head and kissed her softly.

Given how upset she was, it didn't take much for her to lose patience with him. Jenna pulled back and frowned.

"Mustang. Slade could have died. I'm not in the mood for this now."

"I told you, Slade is going to be fine. He may be out of commission right now for what I have in mind for you and me, but he's good." He pushed closer to her, nibbling briefly on one of her earlobes. "Mmm. I was worried you weren't coming tonight you were so late. I'm glad you're here now though."

Mustang's mouth covered hers again, before she pushed him away. "I can't do this."

She glanced back at the doorway to the room where Slade lay unconscious.

His lips traced a path down her throat as his hands headed down to her rear. "I know you're worried, but there's no need. He's only sleeping. Slade sleeps like the dead normally, and between being exhausted from last night with you and groggy from the muscle relaxers the doc gave him, he's totally knocked out. He'll be up and around in a few hours. He can join us then for round two."

Jenna reached down and stilled Mustang's one hand as it headed for the crotch of her jeans. "Really. Mustang. Not now. It would feel like...I don't know...like we're cheating on Slade."

Mustang pulled back and considered Jenna carefully. "For real? That's how you feel?"

Jenna shrugged. "Yeah."

Looking surprised, Mustang let out a soft, "Huh. Interesting."

Jenna frowned. "Why? Don't you feel the same way?"

Mustang laughed and glanced down at the large bulge in his jeans. "Not exactly, no."

She let out a laugh that she didn't know she had in her. "I see that."

One of the riders came down the hall and Jenna took a step back from Mustang. If she was supposed to be Slade's girlfriend, she shouldn't be pressed up against Mustang.

She looked up to find Mustang watching her closely again. "Want me to drive you back to the hotel?"

No. She wanted to see to Slade.

Jenna glanced back at the doorway but before she could say anything, Mustang continued. "They're going to take him to the hospital in a few minutes."

"The hospital?" she squeaked. "You said he was fine."

"For some X-rays." Mustang interrupted her next breakdown. "You don't want to hang around and wait for that. God only knows how long it will take. He'll be in much better shape tomorrow. You can see him then."

"I leave tomorrow." The reality of what that meant struck her hard. She'd leave tomorrow and possibly—probably—never see either Mustang or Slade again.

"What time is your flight?"

"I'm taking a cab to the airport at ten."

"No cab. We'll drive you."

Somehow that made Jenna feel better. Why, she didn't know, since she was still leaving and mostly likely never seeing them again. But they'd be driving her to the airport and she'd get to see for herself that Slade was fine...or at least not dead.

"Will Slade be okay to sit in the car for the drive?"

"Slade?" Mustang laughed. "Darlin', if this wasn't the final night, he'd be on the back of a bull again tomorrow. Hell, I would too if it were me. We bull riders are tough."

As a bull rider limped past, vividly recapping his ride to another cowboy and laughing, even while an icepack was strapped with gauze to his shoulder, Jenna began to fully appreciate just how tough.

"So, will you let me drive you home now?"

"Will you take my cell-phone number and call me if anything changes with Slade?"

Mustang grinned. "Hell yeah. I'll gladly take your cell-phone number, darlin'." As Jenna rolled her eyes, he added, "For Slade. I promise."

"Don't forget, you can call the hotel and get transferred to my room if for some reason my cell doesn't have signal. Right? Just in case?"

Still grinning, Mustang nodded. "Yes, ma'am. I think I can manage that."

With one last glance back at the room's doorway, Jenna sighed and finally nodded. "Okay."

Chapter Twenty

Slade opened the door of the trailer and slowly stepped in with a groan. "God. I feel like I've been run over by a train."

"Bull. Train. Same thing." Lounging in bed, Mustang grinned at Slade. "So what'd they find out at the hospital? Anything?"

"Nothing I didn't already know. Hairline fractures on a couple of ribs. Concussion. The usual."

Mustang pointed to the bandage on Slade's forehead where a hoof had clipped him at some point during Ballbreaker's trouncing. "Did you need stitches for that?"

Slade leaned against the edge of the cabinets, sure he looked as worn out as he felt. "Nah. They used some liquid bandage on it."

"That's good. Wouldn't want a scar to mess up that pretty face of yours." With that, Mustang swung his bare legs onto the floor, grabbed a piece of paper from inside the pocket of the jeans lying crumpled there and thrust it at Slade. "That's for you."

Slade frowned down at the scribbled phone number. "What's this?"

"Jenna's cell-phone number. I thought maybe you'd like to have it."

Slade stared at the slip of paper for a second. When he looked up, Mustang was watching him. "So, you talked to Jenna?"

"Yeah. She somehow got back to the infirmary to see you. I'm not sure exactly how it happened, but it seems as though she got through security by saying she was your girlfriend." Mustang waited as that statement caught Slade's attention.

"She did?"

Mustang nodded. "Yup. Oh, and by the way, I talked to Chase and the kid wants you to know, and I quote, if he had any idea Jenna was with you, he would never have gone anywhere near her in the first place."

Jenna. His girlfriend. *Hmmm.* Slade glanced down again at the number in his hand as he considered that. When he finally raised his eyes, he found Mustang studying him again.

"So, what else happened while I was out of it?" Knowing Mustang, and having seen personally exactly how much Jenna enjoyed Mustang's company the few times they'd all been in bed together, Slade hated to consider the possibilities.

"If you're asking if Jenna and I had sex again without you the answer is no. I tried to take her to bed and she outright refused me."

Slade felt his eyebrows shoot up and consciously wiped the expression from his face.

"That wasn't what I was asking," Slade denied, though it was harder to deny how happy he felt at hearing Jenna had turned Mustang down.

"Yeah, sure it wasn't. Oh, and I told her we'd drive her to the airport in the morning."

Slade's mood did a reversal and turned once more, for the worse, this time at the thought of Jenna flying back to New York. "She's leaving in the morning?"

"Yup, she is. You wanna know something? I've bedded women while I've had broken ribs before. With a dislocated shoulder a time or two too. None of that gets in the way if you pick your positions carefully." Mustang left the unspoken suggestion hanging in the air.

Slade laughed, jarring his sore shoulder and ribs. "You're suggesting we go over there, to Jenna's, now?"

"No. I'm suggesting *you* go over there to Jenna's now. Alone."

Slade drew in a deep breath, immediately regretting it when he felt another painful tug in his ribcage. "Why do you want me to go alone? You have other plans?"

Mustang glanced down at himself. He was in nothing but a T-shirt, boxer shorts and socks. "Do I look like I have other plans?"

Suspicious, Slade pushed further. "Then why don't you want to come with me?"

Mustang shook his head, laughing. "You really don't see it, do you?"

"See what?"

"The way she looks at you. Slade, Jenna's got it bad for you."

"No, she doesn't." If she did, Slade wouldn't have had to bear seeing the satisfied look on her face the many times Mustang had made her come over the last few days. And she wouldn't have been kissing Chase in the arena.

"Yeah, she does. Why else would she turn me down flat tonight?"

"I don't know. She had her reasons I'm sure. Maybe it's her...you know...female time." It was the easiest explanation Slade could come up with, considering.

Mustang laughed. "No, it's not her *female time*. She came right out and said being with me alone would feel like she was cheating on you."

Really? Slade's stomach gave a little jump. "She said that?"

"Yup. Go over to the hotel alone, Slade. See if there really is something there when it's just the two of you. If you don't, I'm afraid you'll regret it."

Slade narrowed his eyes at Mustang. "First of all, when have you *ever* given up a chance to have sex? And second, since when are you such a matchmaker?"

"The answer to the first question is *never*, so you should appreciate my doing so now." Mustang laughed. "As for the second, I guess the answer to that is just now. Right about the time I told you Jenna called herself your girlfriend and you didn't make us pack up the trailer and head for the hills to get away from her."

"I'm not that bad," Slade mumbled.

Mustang raised a brow, silently challenging that answer.

All right, maybe he had been a bit skittish when it came to women recently, but given some of the crazies Mustang liked to bring them, who could blame him? Unfortunately, even if Slade didn't have the instinct to flee, things could still never work out.

Slade felt the need to point that out and remind them both of that fact. "She's leaving for New York tomorrow and we're heading back home to Texas."

"You still have all night tonight before she leaves, and next season's tour kicks off in New York City in only about two months, or did you forget that?"

No, Slade hadn't forgotten. He had actually considered looking Jenna up while they were there, even before Mustang's recent foray into matchmaking.

Before Slade had a chance to say anything in response, Mustang reached again into his jeans on the floor.

"Here." Slade's car keys came flying at him. He reached out and caught them in mid-air with his one good arm as Mustang asked, "You remember which room she's in?"

"Yeah." As if he could ever forget the time they'd spent there last night.

"So, what are you waiting for? Get going."

Slade swallowed hard, scared at how much he wanted to be with Jenna at that very moment. He turned toward the door, and then spun back. "I'll pick you up in the morning and we'll drive her to the airport together. Okay?"

Mustang nodded. "Thanks. I'd like the chance to see her off."

Slade nodded back. Halfway to the door, he heard Mustang call behind him, "Have fun."

"See you in the morning." Slade ignored the flutter in his stomach as he opened the trailer door and headed for his car, and Jenna.

In record time, Slade was standing outside Jenna's hotel room. Heart pounding, he tried to ignore the tremble in his hand as he raised it to knock.

Jenna must have seen him through the peephole, because in no time, he heard the locks flip and the door flew open. "Slade. Thank God."

Then she was in his arms, crying. Slade backed them both into the room, closing the door behind them while he noticed how incredibly good it felt to have Jenna, even a crying Jenna, in his arms.

Damn it. It shouldn't feel so good. After tomorrow she'd be gone. Good thing too, because a city girl from New York and a cowboy from Texas just didn't mix. A few nights were one thing.

A lifetime was another. Jenna was the kind of girl a man was tempted to keep around for a while.

Mustang had been right. At least Slade had tonight. Maybe, hopefully, he and Jenna would have a few more nights in New York when the tour took them there in a couple of months. After that... Well, Slade would have to deal with that later.

In his arms, Jenna pulled back and wiped at her eyes so she could study him from head to toe.

"Are you really okay? You looked so horrible when I saw you lying there in that room." Her voice broke and the tears started again.

"I know. Mustang told me you were upset. That's why I came over." One of the reasons, anyway.

She shook against him as her sobbing continued. Slade pulled Jenna closer, wincing when she clasped her arms around him and squeezed nearly hard enough to break a few more ribs.

"Shh. It's okay, Jenna. I'm fine. Really. Just a few bumps and bruises. Nothing I haven't had before."

Jenna laughed into his chest, which was rapidly growing damp from her tears.

"A few bumps and bruises? Bull riders are crazy."

"Never said we weren't." Slade smiled, stroking her hair and enjoying the feel of her clinging to him since she'd released his ribcage. Now he could feel the benefit of how nicely she was pressed against his crotch. "Jenna?"

She pulled back to look at him with glistening eyes. "Yeah?"

He'd prepared a line about getting naked, but it didn't feel right. Mustang was the king of the lines, not Slade. So instead, Slade did what felt right to him. He tipped his head down and touched his lips to hers.

177

If the room were any darker, he probably would have seen sparks from the electricity coursing through him and into her. Slade claimed Jenna's mouth as his, and she let him. Her hands held him close even as her mouth moved to devour his.

Slade had always loved kissing Jenna before. He liked it even more now that they were all alone with no Mustang between them. Slade wanted Jenna, all of her, naked. Although the silky pajamas she wore certainly felt good, he knew firsthand what was underneath felt even better.

Thankfully, Jenna's mind was in the same place as Slade's. Apparently her goal was also getting them undressed. Jenna unbuttoned his shirt, and then kissed his chest while she reached her hands between them and began to work on his belt. Slade groaned as she conquered not only the buckle, but also his button and zipper.

Slade reached for the buttons on her pajama top just as Jenna slipped one hand inside his briefs and freed him. Then Slade forgot all about his goal of getting Jenna naked as she did something she had never done to him or Mustang before. Jenna pushed Slade down onto the edge of the bed, kneeled between his legs and slid him, all of him, between her lips.

With a groan, Slade watched her make love to him with her mouth. He thought about pulling her up onto the bed so he could please her while she pleased him, but he became transfixed watching her. Slade never meant to let her continue for so long, but it felt so good, before he knew it, he felt the tingling begin.

His whole body tensed and Slade drew in a deep breath. "Jenna. I'm gonna come."

He'd given her fair warning so she could stop if she didn't want him to, but instead, Jenna redoubled her efforts, working him harder and faster. He threw his head back and tried to not finish yet, but it was no use. Finally giving in to the inevitable,

Slade grabbed Jenna's head with both hands, held her still and shouted while she drained him dry.

Only after he'd stopped twitching in her mouth did Slade regain enough sanity to release his grasp on her. He kicked off his boots and pants and pulled Jenna up onto the bed, where they lay next to each other, panting.

He stroked her hair. "Sorry."

Jenna laughed. "Sorry for what? For coming?"

Slade shrugged, regretting the movement immediately when pain shot through his shoulder. He looked down at her face where it lay against his chest. "Yeah, and for coming without, you know, doing anything for you at the same time."

"That's okay." Jenna blushed and bit her lower lip. She looked innocent and devilish at the same time. "I've been kind of wanting to do that to you for a while now. It was nice to concentrate just on you for once. Sometimes multi-tasking is overrated."

He laughed. Who was he to argue with that?

Even though he'd wanted so badly to slide into her from the moment he'd walked in the door, it was probably better off he'd come in her mouth anyway since he hadn't thought to bring protection. The way he'd felt since seeing the concern on her face and feeling her clinging to him, taking Jenna without a condom and saying to hell with the consequences was a definite possibility.

Hell, Slade was still struggling with the urge to slip inside her now and she'd just finished with him.

But his stupidity and the fact he'd forgotten to bring the necessities didn't mean they were done having fun for the night. There was still plenty else they could do and Slade owed Jenna an orgasm. Slipping one hand down inside the elastic waist of her pajama bottoms, Slade felt how wet and warm Jenna was. He wanted her all over again.

Pulling off Jenna's pants, Slade positioned himself between her splayed legs and lowered his head. He heard her sharp intake of breath as his tongue connected with her and he smiled. The way her muscles were already tensing from the smallest touch, Slade predicted he'd have her coming in no time.

Feasting on her, he returned the favor she'd done for him until she was shuddering, writhing and crying out above him. Jenna begged him to stop, saying it was too good and too much, so Slade added his hand and kept going.

Chapter Twenty-One

"Why do you do it? Ride bulls, I mean?" Jenna ran a hand over his chest and felt the warmth of his skin. She cringed inwardly at the purple areas beginning to form on Slade's face and ribs where the bull had pounced on him.

Wearing just the top of her pajamas—her pants were still somewhere on the floor—she leaned over and planted a gentle kiss over the worst of Slade's bruises. He shrugged and then winced. Jenna wondered just how badly it hurt. She didn't bother to ask since he'd never admit to it.

"I don't know. I can tell you this...to this day I remember every heartbeat, every smell, sound and image of my first ride."

Slade was revealing more of himself to her than he ever had before. Jenna asked another question to keep him talking.

"How old were you?"

He stared up blindly, as if he was watching the memory on the ceiling as he retold it.

"I was eighteen the first time I got on a bull. I could tell my buddies were talking to me but it seemed kinda in the distance, you know? When I nodded my head that gate seemed like it took forever to open...slowly creaking wide enough. Then we went on our way." Slade drew in a deep breath and looked at Jenna with a smile. "From there I was hooked. I always wanted to ride after that."

"Wow." Jenna's breath caught at the passion in Slade's softly spoken words.

For the first time she felt like she'd really gotten inside of him. No barriers. No walls. Just Slade, raw, opened wide for her to see. At that moment, she wanted him more than she'd ever wanted anything in her life. She swallowed hard, realizing too that if she didn't clamp down tightly onto her heart right then and there, she'd fall totally in love with this man, the man she'd be leaving in a few hours.

Blinking away the mist that threatened to blur her eyes, Jenna crawled on top of Slade, careful to avoid his shoulder and ribs as she lowered her mouth to his. He lifted both of his hands to encompass her waist as he kissed her back with as much need and desperation as she felt.

Slade rolled them both over and Jenna hissed with concern for his injuries. "Be careful."

He growled as he slid one thigh between her legs. "To hell with careful. I'm fine."

As his mouth covered hers, she didn't argue with him, but when he broke the kiss and cursed, rolling off her again, fear conquered her desire to pull him back on top of her. "What's wrong?"

"I didn't bring protection and you're too damn tempting. I don't trust myself to pull out in time." Slade looked absolutely miserable. "I'm so sorry, Jenna. We can't do this."

"*That's* the only issue? If we had protection we'd be good to...you know."

Slade nodded. "Yes, and I know, I was stupid to forget."

With an evil smirk, Jenna rolled off the bed and grabbed a small white plastic bag off the dresser. She tossed it to Slade on the bed.

"What's this?"

Jenna smiled. "My goody bag from the conference's closing dinner tonight. That's why I was late to the competition. The keynote speaker at the dinner ran late and I was at a table right up front so I really couldn't sneak out in the middle and have everyone see me. Well? Open it."

Looking doubtful, Slade upended the bag. When the contents cascaded onto the bed, his expression changed. Slade picked up and inspected first a condom wrapped up like a lollipop, then a packet of chocolate-flavored lubricant. The elephant-shaped penis warmer got a fairly comical reaction as he read the tag and figured out what it was. He pushed aside the deck of playing cards featuring partially nude, male cover models.

Finally, Slade looked up from the items strewn across the bedspread. "They gave you this kind of stuff at dinner? What kind of conference is this anyway?"

Jenna sat down next to him and picked up a fluorescent green condom from the bed, holding it up between them temptingly. "Are you going to sit around and complain about it or be grateful and make love to me?"

Slade smiled and plucked the packet from her fingertips. "There's no contest there. Though as happy as I am to see this little number, as weird as the color is, I'm a bit intrigued by that chocolate lube. It says it's warming."

Jenna laughed. "We can try that too."

"Oh yeah? Where should we put it?" Slade looked enticingly evil and Jenna felt a tingle spread through her.

She bit her lip as she considered the possibilities she was sure were running through both their minds. "Wherever you want."

In under a minute, Jenna found herself flipped onto her back while on top of her lay a fairly heavy bull rider armed with chocolate lube and a fluorescent green penis. She was totally pinned down and breathless from laughing, but Jenna didn't mind one bit.

What must have been hours later, though it seemed as if she had just closed her eyes after making love with Slade, she heard, "Jenna, baby. We have to get up and go."

She groaned and snuggled deeper beneath the covers. "No. Tired."

Large hands wrapped around her from behind. Jenna felt the warmth of them spreading all the way through her to parts that were nowhere near his fingers. "I know. But we need to pick up Mustang and get you to the airport."

Jenna cracked open an eye and tried to focus on the clock.

"We have time." And she knew exactly how she wanted to use it. A smile spread across her face. "Where is that condom lollipop?"

Jenna heard a deep laugh. "Is that thing usable?"

"Yes." At least she was pretty sure it was anyway. She didn't care either way when, after a few seconds, she felt Slade's erection pressed up behind her.

He slid into her slowly, setting a lazy, gentle pace that was far nicer to wake up to than any alarm clock.

Jenna sighed. "Mmm. I could get used to this."

Slade drew in a deep breath behind her. "Me too."

Slade pulled the car slowly up to the departures drop-off area at Tulsa International Airport and the reality hit Jenna like a slap in the face. She was leaving and would most likely never see either of these men again.

Her throat constricted. Swallowing was almost painful. "So, I guess I better go in."

Slade flung open the driver's side door without looking at her. "I'll get your bags out of the trunk."

Jenna turned to Mustang, who'd been seated to her right for the drive as she squished in the middle of the front bench seat of the car. Jenna hadn't minded the close accommodations between the two men. In fact, considering she'd most likely never be this close to them again, she'd liked it.

She glanced up and found Mustang watching her. "We have your cell-phone number. We'll call later and make sure you got home okay."

Jenna nodded, tempted to point out how she didn't have a cell-phone number for either of them, but then she thought better of it. If she didn't have their numbers, it was because they wanted it that way. She doubted any of their one-night stands, or even three-night stands, had their phone numbers.

The moment Jenna stepped out of that car, she'd be among the ranks of all those who had come before her. She'd be in their past, and a new parade of women would march into their future.

Jenna's sad reverie came to an abrupt end when Slade yanked open Mustang's door and leaned in.

His eyes met Jenna's for the briefest of moments before he pulled them away. She thought she'd seen a hint of sadness or regret, until he addressed Mustang. "We better get moving. The cop's giving me the eye for parking here too long."

He was hinting not so subtly she needed to go. Apparently Slade wasn't having as much trouble with her leaving as she was.

Mustang hauled his large frame out of the door and then leaned down to help her. "We could park and wait with you if you want."

He waited for her to give him the word and she was sure he'd do exactly as he'd offered. She'd like nothing more than to have them wait with her, but why prolong the inevitable? "Nah. It's okay. I have to check in for my flight and then I'll have to pass through security to get to the gate. They won't let you go through with me without a ticket."

Unlike Slade, who had been cold and distant for the entire drive to the terminal, at least Mustang was decent enough to look disappointed at that. He ran his hands up and down her arms. "Jenna, I just want to say I'll never forget this past week and that's entirely because of you."

Oh boy. She was going to cry. She really did not want to do that. Jenna laughed and blinked back the tears. "I can honestly say I'll never forget this week either."

Mustang grabbed her face in both hands and kissed her smack on the mouth. "You kick ass with that book of yours. Okay, darlin'?"

Forget about the stupid book. It was her heart she was worried about.

When Jenna nodded, not trusting her voice, Mustang released her and, after a quick glance at Slade, walked around to the driver's side of the car.

Watching Mustang, Slade frowned. "What are you doing?"

"I'm getting in and starting the car so it looks like we're leaving. That way the cops won't chase us off and you two can take a few minutes to say goodbye."

That left Jenna alone on the sidewalk with her luggage and Slade, who seemed to have eyes for everything except her. He glanced at her suitcase. "Um, so, you got everything, right?"

She patted the laptop case she'd just slipped onto her shoulder and glanced at the large suitcase on wheels standing ready next to her. "Yeah. This is it. Just the two bags."

He nodded. "Okay, then."

Before Slade's big brush off, Jenna had been concerned what the policemen would think if they noticed her kissing two cowboys goodbye. But just as she decided she really didn't care what they thought, it appeared as if Slade might leave her there without so much as a peck on the cheek or even a handshake.

Closer to tears than she had been even during Mustang's touching farewell, Jenna was about to say goodbye and flee to the bathroom to bawl in private when Slade wrapped one strong arm around her, hauled her up close to him and planted a knee-shaking kiss on her mouth. He released her just as suddenly and left her swaying in the aftermath. "Get home safe, Jenna."

Slade grabbed the passenger's side door, slid in and slammed it shut without looking back. Mustang pulled the car away and another vehicle full of travelers instantly pulled in to take its place. The significance of that was not lost on her. She'd be replaced just as quickly in their lives.

Jenna stood watching Slade's car disappear amid the traffic until the hot wetness on her cheeks brought her back to her senses.

She grabbed the handle of her bag and turned. Spotting a curbside check in for her luggage, she managed to thrust the suitcase and her ticket at the attendant without totally losing control. After what seemed like an eternity, he finally finished with the paperwork and usual questions and Jenna was free to go. She stumbled through the sliding glass doors, searching for the sign for the restroom through eyes blurred with tears.

Getting through airport security sucked on a good day but today proved harder than usual. Jenna had grabbed some paper towels from the bathroom, wiped her eyes and gotten in line, only to find she wasn't quite done feeling sorry for herself yet. She had to get out of the line to go back into the restroom and, crushed into a tiny stall with her carry-on hanging from the hook on the back of the door, Jenna let herself get it all out.

Finally, when there were no more tears left, she washed her face and attempted one more time to get through the security inspection without bawling.

Jenna eventually made it through the metal detector, red, puffy eyes and all. Shoeless and jacketless, she was just shoving her laptop back into its bag when she heard a familiar voice and froze. Just a few passengers back stood Lizzie, bitching to a security officer about his not being careful enough with her Author of the Year award.

The perfect addition to a perfectly hellish day.

"No. Please no," Jenna whispered to herself.

"Excuse me?"

Jenna looked up to see the security guard eyeing her. "Um, nothing. It's just this stupid thing never fits back in the bag once I take it out. I'll just carry it and deal with it at the gate."

With another look that suggested she should get the hell out of everyone's way and do just that, he turned to the next person behind her.

Abandoning putting herself back together until she was out of sight of Lizzie, Jenna clutched her laptop to her chest. She grabbed her shoes and jacket in one hand and her laptop bag in the other and, in just her stocking feet, shuffled away as fast as her size six and a half feet could take her.

Jenna located the gate and sunk gratefully into a chair, dumping her armload of stuff on the seat next to her. Systematically, she got her shoes and jacket put back on. She was just deciding if she could bear to look at her pitiful half-written book and try to get some work done during the wait when she looked up and saw a most unwelcome sight.

It seemed the travel gods, much like the love gods, were not with Jenna this week. First, she had the misfortune of getting attached to two cowboys she'd never see again and now, the last person she wanted to spend the next two hours waiting for a flight with was headed right for her.

"Jenna, are you on this flight too?"

She seriously considered denying it but then what would she do when it was time to board? "Hi, Lizzie. Yeah, I am. That's why I'm sitting here at the gate." *Idiot.*

Lizzie planted herself in the seat directly opposite Jenna, then claimed another spot for her Author of the Year award. *Gag.*

Jenna blamed that damn award of Lizzie's for her own willingness to get so drunk at the bar and consequently suck face with a twenty-one-year-old bull rider in the hallway outside the bathroom. Though what had happened when she'd finally returned to her hotel and found Mustang and Slade waiting for her, Jenna didn't regret at all.

That memory of Slade and Mustang led to a return of the feeling of heaviness in Jenna's chest.

"So, I see you have your laptop out all ready to work." Lizzie broke into Jenna's thoughts.

"Yeah, well, you know...deadlines wait for no man."

"I really should do some work too. My editor wants a follow up to my last *New York Times* bestseller ASAP." Jenna scowled, but Lizzie was too self-centered to even notice as she continued on, "So anyway, enough about me."

Yeah, right.

"Tell me. Who were those two hunks in the cowboy hats and the hot muscle car I saw dropping you off?"

Uh oh. "Um..." How much had Lizzie seen? Jenna couldn't say they were her cousins if she'd seen them both kiss her, and not exactly with familial pecks on the cheeks either. Jenna needed a good lie and quick. "I went to college with them both."

"I thought you went to school in upstate New York?"

Dammit. Jenna needed to stop putting so much personal information in her public biography if people like Lizzie were going to use it against her. "Yeah. You know upstate. Tons of farms and horses and stuff. So that's where I met them. We keep in touch, you know, with a letter or a phone call here and there."

Lizzie nodded. "Do they live here in Tulsa?"

Sure. That sounded good. "Yup. They sure do. Big coincidence, huh?"

"Yes, quite." Lizzie laughed and shook her head. "I had a feeling it was something like that. I got off the shuttle from the hotel with Carolina Braun and she swore she recognized them. She said she'd seen them at the bar in our hotel."

Jenna nearly choked. "Really? Hmm. That must have been the night they stopped by to say hi to me."

"Yeah, I figured. Carolina had this whole scenario worked up that you met these strangers at the bar and picked them up. Not just one, but two cowboys. I knew that couldn't be the truth. It sounds more like the plot for a bad romance novel than your life."

No, it sounds like the plot for a great romance novel. Why hadn't she thought of it herself? It was much better than the storyline Jenna had started writing. Even Mustang had known her original story had no potential. Through her bitchiness and passive aggressive, derogatory commentary about Jenna's boring life, Lizzie had given Jenna the perfect idea for her story and she was going to write it, dammit, just as she had lived it.

Jenna laughed aloud at the thought, which earned her a look from Lizzie. Jenna covered by agreeing with her. "Carolina really thought that I picked up two strange cowboys and took them up to my hotel room for some kinky *ménage a trois*? How funny. I guess the risk of being a romance author is that we suffer from overactive imaginations."

"Some do perhaps, but not me. I manage to be able to separate real life and my books."

Jenna ignored Lizzie's smugness and instead flipped open the lid of her laptop. The entire book was right there in her head. She could see it. All she had to do was get it down on paper. Holding her breath with excitement, Jenna opened a new document and began typing.

Ignoring Lizzie, Jenna worked until they announced the last call to board the plane, and even then, she carried the laptop open to her seat. She only closed the lid during takeoff. She had it out again the moment the flight attendant announced they could use approved electronics.

Her fingers couldn't type as fast as her brain fed her the words. The characters, the conflict, the plot points, the story arc... Heart pounding, Jenna realized the story was all right there for the taking.

This was going to be good. No, her book was going to be great. Maybe. *Damn.* Her insecurity started to kick in, but she refused to let it and stomped the doubts back down. It didn't really matter anyway because, good or not, she needed to get this story out of her head and onto paper.

Chapter Twenty-Two

Mustang downed one last sip of beer and stood. "Can I have Jenna's phone number back for a second?"

While he was heading to the bathroom, he might as well use the payphone and call Jenna too. She should have landed by now and he had promised they would call and check on her.

"What? Why?" Slade got unreasonably defensive over Mustang's simple request.

"I want to call and make sure she got home to New York okay."

"I'm sure she's fine." Slade took another sip of his own beer and made no move to give Mustang the number.

"I'm sure she's fine too. But I promised her we'd call. I need her cell number." Slade didn't make a move so Mustang reiterated. "Can I have it, please?"

Slade planted his bottle on the table with enough force to make foam bubble up out of the top. "Why would you promise we'd call her? What the hell were you thinking?"

Blindsided by that insane question, Mustang frowned. "I was thinking that I wanted to make sure the woman we'd just spent the last few days and nights with made it home safely. What the hell, Slade? What is your problem?"

Slade had been cranky and weird ever since they'd left Jenna at the airport.

"My *problem* is that this thing with *us* and her can't go anywhere and by calling her, or even promising to call her, you gave her hope that it could."

Us. The way Slade said that one word caught Mustang's attention. He let it go but stored it away as further evidence that Slade was acting like an ass because he was falling for Jenna.

"That's bull, Slade. Jenna's smart. She's not going to get crazy just because we call to check on her."

"Yes, she will. Women are like that." Slade shook his head. "And what the hell was with that shit you said to her by the car? Was it really necessary for you to lie to her?"

Mustang sighed. "What are you talking about now?"

"*I'll never forget this week because of you, darlin'...*" Slade did a less than flattering imitation of Mustang.

He shook his head. "That wasn't a lie, Slade."

Slade snorted. "Oh, come on. You say that to all the girls we're with."

Not *all* of them, but still Mustang didn't bother to deny it. "Yeah, sometimes I do, and most times it is just a line to keep them happy, but this time it wasn't a lie. Jenna was—*is* special, and you know it as well as I do."

"So what exactly are you saying?" Slade asked accusingly.

Mustang shrugged. "I'm not saying anything. Just that Jenna is different."

"So you mean you want to see her again?"

"Hell yeah. I'd love to see her again and I hope we will both get to when we're in New York." But right now, he'd simply like to keep his promise and call her.

Slade narrowed his gaze menacingly and it suddenly struck Mustang—Slade was acting insane because he was insanely jealous of him. Not only that, Slade was afraid Mustang was falling for Jenna too. Well, that explained quite a bit.

Armed with that knowledge, Mustang could deal with Slade a little better. "You know what, I don't need to call her. Why don't *you* call her?"

"Haven't you been listening to me at all? I'm not calling her. You're not calling her. Nobody is calling her. Besides, I ripped up the damn number and threw it out." Slade picked up his beer again and looked away.

Mustang shook his head at Slade's stupidity. What would happen when Slade eventually got over whatever had crawled up his ass? When he changed his mind and wanted to call Jenna, what was he going to do since he'd thrown out her number?

In the meantime, Mustang had promised to call her and now he couldn't. He knew which carrier she'd flown and what time they'd dropped her off. It probably wouldn't be too hard to call the airline, track down her flight number, and then confirm that the flight had landed safely. It would be a hell of a lot of work to go through just because Slade was an ass. They would know she'd arrived safely, but Jenna would still think Mustang hadn't kept his promise to call her. Perhaps he could track down her phone number through information.

Mustang took one more look at Slade's stone-like expression. He was seriously considering suggesting they drive home to Texas the next day separately but decided to leave well enough alone. It was going to be one hell of a drive in the morning, Mustang feared. The cab of his truck was much too small and Slade's mood far too foul for Mustang to escape the trip unscathed.

Maybe Slade would come up with the idea on his own and offer to drive home in the car while Mustang drove the truck. Slade could drive from Oklahoma to Texas by himself. It wasn't like they were attached at the hip. Slade was a big boy, though he wasn't acting like it now.

But more pressing than tomorrow's drive was that Mustang still had to piss. He sighed and rose from his chair. "I'll be right back."

Slade shrugged, his voice sounding flat. "Yeah. Fine."

Mustang shook his head and turned for the back of the bar. Yup, this was sure gonna be one hell of a drive.

Jenna wrote until the plane landed in New Jersey. She retrieved her car from long-term parking and though she had to drive, she still couldn't keep her brain from thinking about writing the entire distance home from the airport. When she got to her condo, she dumped her suitcase by the door and opened the laptop.

Reliving every moment of the last week, Jenna laughed and she cried. The book, much like her life the past few days, was an emotional roller coaster. She giggled out loud at the scene where her heroine asks the two heroes if they wear a cup when they ride, remembering the looks on Slade and Mustang's faces at that question.

Jenna laughed, knowing she would just as easily cry later on when she wrote the part where the heroine had to leave, but it was okay. Writing this book was kind of like therapy. Being busy kept her mind off missing them. She needed a distraction from the fact they had not called to make sure she'd made it home okay. More than likely they would never call her. She'd never hear their laughs or feel their touch again.

Jenna pushed those thoughts and the pain they caused aside. She sat up and worked on the book until late into the night, or actually, early the next morning. She stopped only to make a cup of tea and then pee.

She wrote until her wrists ached, her back cramped and she couldn't sit any longer. Even then, she put the laptop on the kitchen counter and stood to type for another hour. She only stopped when her eyes finally gave up and refused to focus on the words on the screen any longer.

When Jenna gave in and went to bed, her head continued spinning with snippets of dialogue. She squeezed her eyes shut and willed sleep to come, but her whirling brain wouldn't let it. She fought the temptation to get up again and jot it all down. Finally, she realized it was no use. Jenna got up and scribbled a few lines, and then left the pen and pad of paper next to the bed just in case inspiration struck again during the night—err, rather morning.

Jenna finally fell asleep just as the sun began to creep through her window blinds.

It seemed as if she'd barely closed her eyes when an obnoxious sound, which her exhausted brain took far too long to identify as her cell phone, intruded on her rest. What had she gotten, maybe ten minutes sleep? It certainly felt that way. She could barely focus to see the name on the caller ID.

Thinking it could possibly be the boys calling her, Jenna gave up trying to see who it was and just flipped open the phone instead, but when she heard Astrid's annoyed voice she couldn't help regretting her impulsive choice. On practically no sleep, Jenna was not in the mood to be yelled at by her best friend.

"Why have you been avoiding my calls?"

Jenna stifled a groan as she rubbed the sleep from her eyes. Her voice sounded scratchy when she answered. "I haven't. I left you messages."

"Yeah, on my work phone when you knew I wasn't at work."

"Oh, did I call your work number? Sorry, I just hit your name on my call list. I thought it was your cell." Jenna felt the urge to look out the window and check the sky for lightning bolts at that whopper of a lie. Although, she was pretty impressed with herself for coming up with it so fast, especially given her current, sleep-deprived state.

Jenna could practically hear Astrid's frown through the phone. "How come you never answered when I called you?"

"I've told you what these conferences are like, Astrid. I can't answer the phone in the middle of a session or a speech, can I? They keep us on the go from early morning until late at night." Not to mention the extracurricular activities that Jenna had managed to fit in on her own in the off hours.

"Did you at least get out to see Tulsa? One of my co-workers told me there are some beautiful art deco buildings downtown. There's supposed to be a Frank Lloyd Wright house too."

Normally, Jenna would have been into all of that, but this trip, she was more into seeing her country boys than seeing the country. "Nope. The only sightseeing I did was what I saw from the back seat of a cab between the airport and the hotel."

"Oh really? And yet you managed to go out and meet those two bull riders on your birthday. Which you never told me about, by the way."

Jenna sighed and got ready for another round of stretching the truth. "I went to the sports complex to watch the bull-riding competition for my book research and then I met them at the place across the street afterward to get back my manuscript, which they had fact checked for me. I had exactly one drink. That's it, Astrid."

Jenna eyed the original manuscript, the one Slade had corrected for her. It lay on the table where she'd left it after going through and highlighting any bull facts he'd penciled in that she thought she could use for the new book. In between the romance she did want to include some bull riding, and Slade had given her some great details, not to mention his soul-touching recollection of his first ride. That was definitely going in the book.

"And? How did you leave it with your two rodeo cowboys? Are you going to keep in touch with them to get more stuff for your book?"

"I didn't get either of their phone numbers." Jenna pouted, because amid all the lies she'd been spewing recently, that part was sadly the absolute truth.

"You let them go without getting their numbers? Oh my God, Jenna. Have I taught you nothing?"

"What was I supposed to do? They didn't offer to give me their numbers." But they did have her number. Although, since they hadn't called to see that she'd landed safely like they'd promised, if they called her at all it would be a miracle.

With that depressing thought, Jenna listened to Astrid lecture her some more while she pulled her laptop from under the bed. Snuggling under the covers, she booted up and opened the file for her new book, typing as quietly as possible while, hopefully, responding with an occasional "mmm hmm" or "you're right" at the appropriate times during Astrid's monologue.

Chapter Twenty-Three

The phone rang and Jenna saw her agent's name on the caller ID. Heart pounding, she answered the call with hands that trembled. "Hello."

"I love it."

The breath Jenna had been holding whooshed out of her in one huge burst. "You do? Really?"

"It's exactly what the publishers are looking for. Cowboys, lots of hot sex, a male-female-male ménage. It's perfect."

Thank God. "Thanks, Marge."

"I would make one suggestion, though."

Here it comes. Jenna's heart fell as far as it had lifted just moments before. "What's that?"

"I'm submitting this one to the publisher as it is, but you might want to consider making it a true ménage for your next book."

She stowed the rejoicing over Marge's talking about her next book and frowned. "What do you mean a *true* ménage?"

There couldn't be much more sex in there. She had the characters doing pretty much everything possible. Parts lower warmed at the memory that she too had done pretty much everything possible with her two cowboys in real life. Damn, she missed them.

"You know. Male-male-female. The hottest sellers right now are books where the men have a sexual relationship with each other, as well as with the woman."

Jenna felt the color drain from her face as she considered what Slade and Mustang would think if she wrote a sexual relationship for their two characters in the book. She didn't think their reaction would be pretty.

"Uh, okay. I'll keep that in mind. Maybe for the next book..." One about totally fictional cowboys, not real bull riders who would be very unhappy with her.

"Good. Because I think you've got the beginnings of a whole line of rodeo-themed, western romance ménages here. Your details are great."

"It's not a rodeo."

"Hmm?"

"It's not..." Jenna heard the rustling of papers on Marge's desk and realized the limited window of Marge's attention span had expired. "Never mind. Um, so what's the next step?"

"You get to work and start writing the next book. I'm confident this manuscript will not only get contracted, but they'll probably want to contract the next one or two in the series in advance. Can you come up with stories for the side characters?"

"A contract for a series? Wow. Yeah, sure I can come up with more stories."

"Great, because there's a good chance this book will be a bestseller for you."

Bestseller. Jenna's heart sped at the words.

"Listen, my other line is ringing. I'll get a contract for this manuscript to you the moment they make an offer, which shouldn't take long."

"Okay. Thanks."

As Marge hung up, Jenna wanted nothing more than to call Mustang and Slade and tell them about the book and her agent's reaction to it, but she couldn't. They hadn't called her, and she couldn't call them. That overshadowed everything else.

Frustrated, Mustang gripped the phone tighter and tried to rein in his annoyance with the operator on the line. Who would have thought finding one little phone number could be so hard?

Chase rounded the corner and donned a huge smile. "Hey, Mustang. Can you believe we're actually in New York City?"

Showing Chase the receiver of the payphone he held to his ear, Mustang frowned at the rookie and held one finger up against his own lips just as the operator's voice came back on the line and asked him to spell Jenna's name.

"Jenna Block. B-l-o-c-k... No, I guess I'm not sure which city she lives in. I'd thought it was New York City... No, I didn't know there were five different boroughs in New York City. Can't you check all of them? Or actually, you better check the whole state." Maybe she didn't live in the city. She'd never actually said she did, he'd just assumed.

Mustang stared impatiently at the scratches in the acrylic partition surrounding the hotel lobby's payphone as he waited. For some reason, Chase stood there and waited with him. Mustang opened his mouth to ask the kid why just as the patronizingly helpful voice on the other end of the line gave him an absurdly high number of J. and/or Jenna Blocks living in New York State and what little hope he had of tracking down Jenna while they were in New York faded.

Mustang ran a hand over his face and resisted the urge to beat his head against the wall. "Oh. That many, huh? Okay. Never mind. Thanks."

With a huge sigh, he slammed the receiver back onto the cradle with more force than was necessary. At a loss what to try next, he turned to go back up to his room only to find Chase watching him.

"Doesn't Slade have Jenna's phone number?"

"It's complicated, kid." Mustang walked away, but Chase followed. Puppies and young bull riders tended to follow Mustang around. He'd never quite understood why.

"What happened? Did Slade lose her number? Oh, man, is she gonna be pissed off at him."

More likely Slade was gonna be pissed at Mustang, possibly enough to beat the crap out of him, when he found out about Mustang's meddling.

Slade had torn up and thrown away Jenna's phone number for a reason, though most likely not for the reason Slade had given. He'd said it was so Mustang couldn't call Jenna and give her false hope. Mustang had another theory. He was convinced Slade got rid of that number because he was too tempted to call her himself.

Mustang was starting to grasp that, when it came to self-denial and stupid choices, Slade was a real champ. Ranked number one.

Stopping when he finally reached the bank of elevators, Mustang realized the kid was still trailing behind him. He turned with a sigh, hoping the rookie wouldn't follow him all the way up to his room.

"What I don't get is why you're trying to find Jenna's number instead of Slade. I mean, she was dating him, not you."

This kid really needed to learn when to leave well enough alone. "Slade's too damn stubborn, that's why."

Chase stood before him, smiling. Mustang wasn't in the mood for anyone who was smiling.

The elevator door slid open and Mustang took a step toward it, looking forward to putting some distance between himself and Rookie Smiley.

"So, I guess it's lucky for Slade I can get him Jenna's number. Huh?"

Chase's statement stopped him dead in his tracks.

"You can?" The elevator doors closed again and Mustang made no attempt to stop them, suddenly not so annoyed with Chase any longer.

"Yeah, I'm pretty sure I can get her number, or at least get a message to her."

"How?" Had Jenna given her number to Chase back in Tulsa? This was too good. Why didn't Mustang think to ask the kid right away instead of going to all that trouble calling directory assistance trying to track her down on the damn payphone?

"When Jenna and her friends were at the bar in Tulsa, one of the other authors, Barb was her name, hooked up with Garret James. Garret got Barb's number and they've been texting back and forth since that night. He could ask Barb for Jenna's number. I bet she's got it."

For a man who had yet to give in and buy a cell phone, it all sounded intriguing but also pretty complicated to Mustang. Luckily, Chase didn't seem concerned as he whipped out his cell phone and punched a few buttons. Not more than a few seconds later, the damn thing chimed.

Chase glanced at it, then looked up from the phone grinning. "Garret says he'll text Barb and ask for Jenna's number right now. He'll get back to me when he has it."

Skeptical, Mustang crossed his arms and leaned against the wall, waiting. Lo and behold, about a minute later, Chase's phone chimed again. The kid read the screen and then thrust the phone at Mustang for him to see the digits for himself.

"There you go. Jenna's number. Want me to dial for you?"

Mustang stared at the phone in Chase's hand for a second, considering. Finally, he sighed.

What the hell. Why not?

How bad could Slade hurt him anyway? He could do no worse than what Mustang got every time he jumped on the back of a bull.

Decision made, he nodded. "Yeah. Go ahead. Call her."

After a few static-filled rings, the voice Mustang hadn't heard for months came through the phone. "Hello?"

Mustang swallowed, strangely nervous. "Hey, darlin'."

There was a moment of silence followed by a short laugh that didn't sound at all happy. "Mustang." She'd recognized his voice too.

This may take a bit of charm. "That's right. The one and only. How have you been, darlin'?"

"Fine."

Chase had been dead on. Judging by the one-word answers, Jenna was pissed as all hell because they hadn't called.

"How would you like a chute-side ticket to watch a bull ride at Madison Square Garden?"

She was silent and Mustang wished, not for the first time, that he wasn't beholden to Chase for the use of his phone. He really wanted the kid to go away so he could have some privacy to talk with her and maybe explain things.

Jenna was quiet for so long Mustang finally asked, "Uh, hello?"

"I'm here." He heard her blow out a long breath of air. "What day?"

Mustang grinned. "Tomorrow night. Eight pm. I'll leave the ticket under your name at the pick-up window."

Again, she took a long time to answer. "All right."

"Okay, great. See ya then, darlin'."

"Okay. Bye." Then the call went dead.

Mustang took a deep breath and handed the phone back to Chase.

It looked like Jenna was going to require some soothing. Getting back in her good graces and her bed was going to be a lot of work.

Damn Slade.

Chapter Twenty-Four

Slade glanced down at the tattered scrap of paper he held between two fingers. The ink was so worn and faded from being carried around in his wallet for months that the numbers were barely visible.

He couldn't count how many times he had taken this paper out and considered calling her. But this time he wasn't a thousand miles away and calling her didn't seem as pointless.

Steeling his nerves, he sat on the edge of the mattress and reached for the phone on the nightstand between the room's two double beds.

He'd dialed three numbers when he heard the door unlock and open. Slade slammed the receiver down and stood, hiding the paper deep in the front pocket of his jeans just as Mustang walked into the room.

Slade shoved his hands into his pockets and tried to look casual. "So, uh, what's up?"

"Not much." Mustang barely glanced at Slade, making a beeline directly for the remote control.

Slade breathed freer when all of Mustang's concentration focused on the television as it sprang to life. Slade sat again, stretching his legs out on the ugly bedspread as he heard the cheesy music of the hotel's information channel come on.

He couldn't call Jenna if Mustang stayed planted right here all night. He glanced at the clock. "So, you got anything planned for later?"

Mustang shook his head, eyes still on the television as he clicked through the cable channels. "Me? Nope."

"Any of the other guys doing anything?"

Mustang nodded. "The kids are all going out barhopping for the night. Hey, look. We've got two movie channels."

"Don't you want to go out with them?" Slade had been hopeful, but Mustang's discovery of HBO sunk any chance that he'd leave the room.

Glancing over at Slade, Mustang answered, "Not really. Do you?"

"Nah. I don't wanna be hung over for tomorrow."

"Yeah, me neither. Not for the first match up of the season after being off for so long."

It appeared as if they were at a standoff, Mustang not leaving the room, Slade not willing to give in and go find a payphone. That was okay. Slade figured he could wait him out until Mustang casually added, "Oh, and Jenna's going to be in the audience tomorrow."

Slade's head whipped around to glare at Mustang. "What?"

Still staring at the television, Mustang didn't react one bit to the harshness of Slade's single growled word. "Jenna. I left her a ticket in the VIP section for tomorrow."

"You called Jenna?"

Did Mustang have Jenna's number all this time and Slade's whole charade of pretending to throw it out was for nothing? Finally, Mustang met his gaze.

"Actually, Chase did." And as Slade nearly choked on that, Mustang laughed. "Yeah, I thought you'd react like that."

"Chase had Jenna's phone number?"

"It was on his phone." Mustang shrugged and went back to flipping channels.

Slade frowned, no longer in the mood for talking or much of anything else. He couldn't get the thought out of his head, though. Jenna had given Chase her number. *Shit.*

✳

Booty call.

That was the only term Jenna could come up with to describe the way Mustang and Slade had ignored her for months and then called her now that they were in New York. They wanted to sleep with her again.

And she had agreed to meet them. She let out a bitter laugh. What the hell did that say about her?

The more she thought about it, the angrier she got. Finally, she grabbed her cell phone, found the number Mustang had called from in her incoming call log and hit the send key.

When she heard the "hello" through the receiver, she laid into him. "Why did you wait so long to call me?"

"Huh? Who is this?"

That figured. He didn't even know who she was. Though it was no wonder. Who knew how many girls called him day and night? She let out a loud, frustrated breath. "It's Jenna."

Jeez. He'd just talked to her.

"Jenna. Hey. This is Chase."

"Chase?" Why the hell was Chase answering Mustang's phone?

She heard him laugh. "Yup. It's me. How are you?"

Now that she really listened, Jenna heard the difference in Chase's voice compared to Mustang's, something she hadn't noticed during the start of her why-haven't-you-called-me hissy fit.

"Um, I'm well, thanks. And you?"

"Well, I'm wearing my Rookie of the Year buckle, I'm in New York City for the first time in my life and I'm riding tomorrow night at Madison Square Garden. I'd say life is pretty good."

"Yeah, it sounds like it."

Chase's youthful exuberance was infectious. Jenna couldn't help but smile.

"So how did that super secret book you were researching in Tulsa turn out?"

"Really good actually." Jenna didn't go into the details for many reasons, but finishing on time and getting a contract soon definitely qualified as really good. Especially considering how badly her first attempt at the cowboy book had gone.

"That's great."

Jenna could hear the smile in his voice and laughed. He really was excited for her. "Actually, I already started writing another one."

"Is this one about bull riders too?"

"Yes. It's about a young rookie bull rider with a taste for older women." Jenna felt herself blush and waited for Chase's reaction.

"No way. Really?"

Jenna smiled. "Really."

She heard Chase laugh. "Wow, that's great. I'm gonna have to read that one."

Of course, he thought it was great. Chase could get enthused about pretty much anything. Compared to the stuck-up, self-centered idiots Astrid encountered online and kept trying to fix her up with, Chase was refreshing, to say the least. If only Jenna were ten, all right, maybe fifteen years younger...

"You? Reading a romance novel? That should go over well with the other bull riders," she teased him.

"Eh, they won't care. Especially when they hear I know you and that I kind of inspired it. I did, didn't I?"

"Yes, you did." Jenna laughed, flashing back to their make-out session in the bar in Tulsa and feeling her cheeks heat. Speaking of Tulsa... "Um, Chase, why are you answering Mustang's phone?"

That elicited another laugh from Chase. "Actually, Mustang called you on my phone. Mustang and Slade both don't have cell phones."

"What? Are you serious? Why not?"

"Well, the story from the old timers is that in the beginning they weren't making enough money riding to pay the phone bills. Then it became kind of a thing with them. Holding out and not getting one even though they could afford to if they wanted. Making fun of the rest of us for texting or being on our phones all the time. You know?"

Jenna shook her head. "Just like how they sleep in the trailer rather than in a hotel."

Chase laughed. "Yeah, just like that. Though they're in a hotel here. They flew in. No good place to park the trailer this competition."

"Hmm. I guess not." Jenna felt strangely sad at that. There was a special place in her heart for that trailer. Then she thought of something. "What hotel are you guys in?"

Chase told her the name. "Why? You wanna come over and visit?"

Jenna laughed. "No. I don't think so."

"Don't be mad at Slade, Jenna."

This kid was far too perceptive. "What makes you think I'm mad?"

"The way you laid into me when I answered the phone and you thought I was Mustang made me think you're not too happy with him and Slade right now. But you shouldn't be mad."

"Okay, hypothetically, let's assume I am mad. Why shouldn't I be?"

"You didn't hear this from me, but in answer to your hypothetical question, Mustang told me Slade lost your number. That's why he didn't call you."

Jenna's eyes blurred with tears of relief. Slade was a clumsy idiot for losing her number, but that was far better than the assumption she'd been under for months now, that neither one of them wanted to ever talk to her again. "Oh. Thanks for telling me, Chase."

"No problem. Just don't tell them I told you."

She smiled. "No problem."

"So, I heard Mustang say you're coming to watch us ride tomorrow night."

Jenna cleared the emotion from her throat. "Yeah, that's the plan."

"Good. I'll look for you in the stands and say hi."

"I'd like that."

"I hate to cut you short, Jenna, but the guys are outside waiting for me to catch a cab with them. We're going to some seaport place."

Jenna smiled. "South Street Seaport?"

"Yeah. That's it."

"Okay, but be careful and only use the yellow taxi cabs. Any other ones are unregulated. Don't use those. Okay?" Those gypsy cab drivers would take one look at a bunch of sweet young cowboys and triple the price.

"Yellow cabs only. Got it. Thanks, Jenna. I'll see you tomorrow?"

"Yes, you will. Good night, Chase."

"Night, Jenna."

Jenna closed her cell phone and rubbed her eyes as she digested all she'd just learned.

They hadn't given her their cell phone numbers because they didn't own any. If she'd heard it from anyone besides Chase, who probably wouldn't be able to tell a lie even if he tried, she wouldn't have believed it.

Suddenly, Jenna had to rethink everything she'd felt over the last few months concerning Slade and Mustang. But first, she had something she needed to do. Jenna squatted down and pulled a box out from underneath her bed. From inside, she grabbed a photocopy of her cowboy book.

Jenna drew in a big breath, letting it out again slowly as she ran a hand over the cover page. Her heart and soul were contained within those pages. Sending it to the boys would be equivalent to confessing everything she felt about them, about their time together, the hurt, the love, the sex...

She stayed frozen on her knees in front of the ream of paper for a long time.

Nothing ventured, nothing gained. Besides, being a writer, if it turned out they didn't feel the same about her, she'd deny the whole thing and call it fiction.

"Chicken," her subconscious yelled.

"Protecting yourself," the sissy side of her countered.

Let her self-doubt say whatever it wanted. Jenna grabbed her purse and her coat and headed for the door.

She paused, manuscript in hand. She could drive into the city and leave it at the hotel desk, but she was already shaking just from speaking with Mustang. She wasn't about to fight the traffic on the bridge and in midtown Manhattan in this state of mind. Besides, she'd never be able to find a spot on the street near their hotel to park. Taking a train there and back would take forever. It would be really late by the time she got home.

Jenna glanced at her watch. The shipping place was still open. She'd overnight the package to the boys. It would be cheaper to ship it than pay for tolls and parking anyway.

They would have it in their hands by ten the next morning. Then, by the time she saw them at the Garden the next night... Jenna stopped, her hand still on the doorknob as she pulled it shut behind her.

Then what? She considered what she wanted out of this strange but wonderful relationship with the two cowboys. More importantly, what did they want?

Whatever it was, they'd deal with it, the three of them together.

That resolved, Jenna headed for the elevator. She'd get the package mailed and then she had to get home and figure out what to wear to a bull ride in Manhattan. That was a hell of a fashion dichotomy. Good thing Jenna enjoyed a challenge. She must. She was about to take on two cowboy playboys.

Chapter Twenty-Five

His gear bag held in one hand, Slade walked into Madison Square Garden and took in the enormity of the cavernous arena.

It didn't matter that he was far from being a rookie anymore, or that he had ridden there many times before, it still hit him each and every time he entered exactly how huge it was for a kid who grew up poor in Texas to be riding in one of the most famous arenas in the country.

Slade rubbed a spot located somewhere between the bottom of his ribcage and his belt buckle, trying to will away the fluttering there. Why the hell was he nervous? He knew—he just didn't want to admit it.

Dammit. Slade was exactly where he wanted to be. Riding in the pros. Ranked number two in the world. Supporting himself doing what he loved and, God willing, he'd stay healthy enough to continue to do so. He should be on the top of the world, and yet he had never felt more uncertain about things in his life. All because of one brown-haired, hazel-eyed city girl and her book about falling for two cowboys.

Mustang jogging up next to him interrupted his reverie.

"I just checked. The box office has Jenna's ticket held for her so we're good to go."

Good to go. Yeah, right.

Slade glanced at the empty stands, eyeing the section where last year, before he had ever heard the name Jenna Block, his teammates' girlfriends and wives had been seated.

He and Mustang had arrived early so the stands were still empty, but soon amid thousands of fans would be Jenna, sitting somewhere in that VIP section. No doubt she'd be in the front row in a seat directly behind the chute. There she would be as distracting as possible, thanks to the ticket Mustang had left for her. After Chase had called her.

There were far too many men in Jenna's life for Slade's liking. Mustang. Chase. And those were only the ones he knew about. Who knew how many more were chasing after her in New York. But Jenna wasn't his, so how could he be mad at anything Mustang, or Chase, or any other man did regarding her?

Slade's hand moved up to rub a spot on the left side of his chest as he considered that. He thought about the ending of the book where the main character can't choose between the two cowboys and asks them both to be with her. How much of Jenna was in that book and how much was made up? The question had been eating him up since he'd read it. His hand moved down to rub his aching gut.

"What's up with you tonight?"

Slade turned to Mustang, who was watching him. "Nothing's up. Why?"

"You're nervous. I can see it on your face. Hell, it's written all over your body. You're acting like...I don't know, some virgin bride on her wedding night."

Slade cocked one brow at that comparison. "I haven't been a virgin in a very long time, Mustang."

"Maybe your dick hasn't been, but your heart still is."

In no mood for Mustang's philosophical riddles right now, Slade shook his head. "What's that supposed to mean?"

"Think about it."

Slade let out a sigh. "I don't have time for word games. I gotta rosin up my rope."

"Yeah, I have to do that too." Mustang moved to follow Slade and then stopped. "You want to be alone or can I come?"

Slade frowned. "What the hell are you talking about now? Why would I need to be alone to get my rope ready?"

Mustang shrugged. "I don't know. Just asking. You've been acting so strangely lately, I thought maybe you'd want privacy or something."

"You keep this weird shit up and I might." Slade scowled and headed for the locker room to drop his bag and get himself ready, mentally and physically, before Jenna arrived and shot his concentration all to hell.

Mustang was an idiot Slade could ignore, he'd had enough practice doing it, but seeing Jenna again for the first time in months, that was going to be harder for Slade to put out of his mind.

Time never passed so slowly as when you were waiting for something. Slade checked the clock more times than he could count. He prepped his rope for far longer than necessary. He even checked out the bulls back in the stock pens, something he hadn't done since before he began riding pro, back when he had no idea what kind of bull he'd get in the draw.

Finally, Slade forced himself to sit down and try to relax, until he heard the typical noises of the crowd starting to fill the arena. Then relaxing was out of the question.

Not long now. Elbows braced on his knees, Slade buried his face in his hands and tried to scrub away the tension.

"I knew she'd come."

Slade looked up and found Mustang standing in front of him, grinning.

"Jenna's here?"

Mustang nodded. "Yup. Come on. Let's say hello."

Slade swallowed and his heart rate doubled. "We aren't supposed to go out before we've been introduced during the big opening."

Mustang bent down and started unbuckling his chaps. He took off his vest and pulled his hat down low over his eyes. "There. Now no one will know who I am."

Mustang waited for Slade to do the same.

Drawing in a big breath and letting it out very slowly, Slade stood. He stripped off anything that had a sponsor logo on it and then wiped the sweat from his palms onto his jeans. "Okay. Let's go."

The "virgin bride" comment kept running through Slade's head as he realized his hands were trembling. *Shit.*

If he'd read into that book correctly, Jenna was telling them she was theirs for the taking, both of them if they wanted. What the hell did he want? Slade considered that as they drew closer to Jenna.

Then, before he knew it, Mustang had grabbed Jenna's hand and was pulling her out of her seat. There was no more time for Slade's agonizing over what he did or didn't want, because the object of his ponderings was right in front of him, melting him from the inside with one glance.

"Mustang. Slade." Jenna smiled and set Slade's stomach fluttering.

"Shh. We're incognito, darlin'. Come on."

"Where are we going?"

Mustang grinned down at her, then at Slade. "Someplace where we can say a proper hello."

Slade swallowed, his mouth suddenly dry as he anticipated Jenna's lips beneath his, his hands on her body. Mustang led the pack, dragging Jenna by the hand behind him. Slade followed willingly, wondering where they were going but not caring all that much as long as they got there, and alone, fast.

With a glance over his shoulder, Mustang pushed through a door marked *No Admittance* and the three found themselves in a long and, thankfully, empty hall.

"Damn, I've missed you." Mustang shook his head and smiled at her. "You look better than I remember."

Jenna's eyes shot to Slade and then back to Mustang. "I've missed both of you too. A lot."

His eyes still on Jenna, Mustang said, "Slade, come on over here and give Jenna a proper hello."

Mustang angled himself and made room, and Slade took a step forward. He somehow found his voice. "Hi."

Jenna peered up at him with the same look in her eyes he'd last seen that night in her hotel room when she'd picked up the green condom and pretty much dared him to use it.

Next to him, Mustang ran a hand up and down the arm of Jenna's black sweater. "Darlin', I hope you don't think me rude, but if I don't kiss you this minute, I think I may die."

Glancing quickly at Slade, she laughed before answering Mustang. "I know exactly how you feel."

"Good to hear." Mustang lowered his head and his mouth covered hers. Slade watched—envious, wanting—until Jenna's hand reached out and grabbed a fistful of his shirt. She reeled him in, broke from Mustang's mouth and leaned up to touch her lips to his.

He sank into her kiss, feeling like he'd come home.

When she pulled away, he had only one thing to say. "Jenna."

She smiled. "I heard you have a hotel room this time. I hope it's close."

Next to him, Mustang laughed. "Close enough."

"Good. But we better get out of here before we get in trouble." Jenna turned toward the door then stopped. "You do have condoms in your hotel room, I hope. If not, one of you better stop somewhere after the competition."

Mustang's laugh echoed off the walls of the empty hall as they followed her toward the door. "Don't worry, darlin'. I got it covered."

Slade let out a long slow breath as Jenna pushed through the door ahead of them. "Wow."

Mustang laughed. "You can say that again."

✳

Slade stood, one boot up on the rail, the other on the ground, and huffed out a breath.

"Soon," Mustang said softly next to him.

Slade allowed himself a glance in the direction of Jenna's seat in the stands. "Not soon enough."

"Just relax."

Slade shot Mustang a look. "I am relaxed."

One brow rose up beneath Mustang's hat as he stared pointedly at Slade's hand. Slade had been drumming out a loud, impatient, tuneless rhythm on the rail without even realizing it. He stilled his fingers. "Sorry."

"I've never seen you like this over a girl."

"Who says it's over a girl?" *Liar.*

Mustang let out a snort. "It sure as hell ain't over that bull you drew. My grandmother could ride him."

Mustang's grandmother may well have been riding that night. Slade wouldn't have known either way. He had no attention for what was happening in the arena, except to wish it would go faster.

Forty-five bulls and riders took a long time to get loaded into the chutes one at a time, and since Mustang was ranked fourth and Slade second, it meant they had to cool their heels and wait around for almost all of the others to ride before them. It also meant that Slade was crawling out of his skin to get his ride over with. Mustang was correct. Slade's anxiety had nothing to do with nerves over his ride.

He dared to glance in Jenna's direction again and let out a nearly feral growl at the sight that greeted him. "God damn that kid."

Mustang turned to look, then laughed. "Hey, if it wasn't for Chase, she wouldn't even be here. He got us her number, remember."

Remembering that pissed Slade off even more, but he kept his mouth shut since he wasn't about to tell Mustang he'd had Jenna's number all along. He'd just been too stupid, or too stubborn... Hell, maybe he'd just been too afraid to use it. No matter what the reason, he wasn't feeling up to confessing any of that to Mustang right now, if ever. It was hard enough facing those realizations himself.

He glanced up and saw Mustang laughing at him.

"You keep giving me nasty looks like that and I might not tell you what I was about to tell you."

Slade shook his head, scowling. "I guess I won't be hearing it then."

"You sure? You'll like it. Aren't you the least bit curious?"

"Nope." Shit, he was curious now. Slade hated that. He said as casually as he could muster, "All right, just get it out of your system. I know you're dying to."

Mustang laughed. "Yeah. You want me to tell you for my benefit, and not for yours."

"Fine, don't tell me then. I don't care."

Mustang had always acted like a juvenile, but when exactly had Slade started acting like a child right along with him? Oh, yeah. Right about the time he developed the schoolboy crush on Jenna.

"I know I let you believe Jenna gave Chase her phone number, but she didn't."

"What?"

Mustang grinned wider. "Yup. He got it from a friend of hers who hooked up with Garret that night she was out drinking with them all in Tulsa. Remember?"

Slade remembered. Hell, he'd never forget any part of that night, or any of his time in Tulsa. "What the hell, Mustang? Why did you let me think she gave her number to Chase?"

Mustang had purposely let him go on believing Chase had been talking to Jenna for the past two months.

"Because it was fun."

Slade shot a nasty look at Mustang's profile. "Yeah, real fun."

"How many women were you with during the off-season, Slade?"

Holy crap! Where had that question come from?

Slade glanced around to make sure no one else had heard. "That's none of your business."

Mustang frowned. "Jeez, Slade. We've been inside the same girl at the same time. Don't act like I'm invading your privacy or something. Just answer the damn question."

They weren't even halfway through the lineup so it wasn't like Slade could be saved by having to get ready to ride. Mustang and his question weren't going anywhere so he might as well answer.

Slade avoided eye contact. "None."

"None," Mustang repeated, looking satisfied with himself. "See. Don't you realize what that means?"

"Not really, no."

"I can't count how many girls I was with over the past two months."

"Like that's something to brag about?" Slade scowled.

Mustang laughed. "I'm not bragging. I'm trying to prove a point. Slade. Listen to me. Yeah, I like Jenna. A lot. But I was with other girls after her and you weren't. You're in love with Jenna."

Slade narrowed his eyes at that accusation. "I don't love her."

"You sure as hell do. I can see it. You seem to be the only one who can't."

"I'll admit I like her."

"Fine. Call it whatever makes you happy, but actions speak louder than words."

"What actions? If you're talking sex, you've had as much of that with her as I have."

"Not exactly, since you had that one night alone with her before she left Tulsa, but I'm not talking about sex anyway. I mean the way you were ready to kill Chase for just looking in her direction. The way you never really liked sharing her even with me."

"I—" Slade tried to interrupt to deny that but Mustang barreled right over him.

"No. Let me finish. Don't you see, Slade? I don't feel the same way. I have no problem with you and her spending the night together with or without me there. Hell, I wouldn't have had a problem if she'd taken Chase to her bed."

Slade felt ill as that image twisted his gut.

Mustang continued. "I shouldn't feel like that, should I? I mean, she's fun and smart and I love spending time with her and the sex... Well, you know, that is always amazing..."

"Okay, enough. I get it."

Mustang laughed. "See. You're proving my point. I obviously don't feel the way you do about her."

Slade blew out a breath. "That might be true. Maybe I like her more than you like her."

"And that's exactly why you need to start taking this thing to the next level."

Slade laughed. "What next level? We've already done pretty much everything a man and woman can do together, Mustang." With a few exceptions he wouldn't mind trying.

"I'm talking about a date. Ask her out. Start a relationship. Think of her as a girlfriend because it's more than obvious to me, and should be to you too, she is way more than a one-night stand."

That much was true. "What about Jenna?"

"What about Jenna?" Mustang asked.

Slade kicked at the floor with the toe of his boot, trying to find the words. "I think it's pretty obvious she likes being with you too."

"In bed, you mean?"

Slade lowered his voice even further. "Both in bed and out. You make her laugh." The pain of that statement cut through Slade's heart, confirming Mustang's accusation that Slade probably did like—he wasn't going to say *loved*—Jenna too much for his own good.

"You'd make her laugh if you didn't go all stone faced whenever we're together. And as far as the bed part...we can work around that."

Slade's brow shot up. "Work around that how?"

"Well, it's not like we haven't all already been together, you know? There is nothing to stop her from being your girlfriend exclusively, but I could still, uh...*join* you two on occasion, if you wanted me to."

No, Slade did *not* want Mustang *joining* him and Jenna in bed, but he feared Jenna might want exactly that.

Mustang laughed. "You're not too fond of that idea, are you? Your face looks like you just bit into a lemon."

For once, Mustang was right. Slade wasn't fond of the idea and the acid backing up his throat might as well have been raw lemon juice. Just like the bad taste in his mouth, Slade found it hard to swallow the idea of sharing Jenna with Mustang once she'd become truly his girl. His pride wasn't swallowed any easier, but he forced it down anyway. "All right."

Mustang's eyes opened wide. "All right what?"

Slade let out a bitter laugh at the realization that to keep Jenna happy, he'd do just about anything, no matter how distasteful. "If that's what Jenna wants, then yeah, I guess I'd have to work with it."

Mustang laughed and Slade looked up and saw his friend shaking his head. "What?"

"Just watching you, looking so miserable, I kinda hope I don't find the one for quite a while. I'm happy just the way I am." Mustang slapped Slade on the back. "I think we all fall eventually. I'm just happy you fell first."

Slade glanced at the arena clock, wishing this night over already so they could get to Jenna. Even if he would be sharing her with Mustang, just thinking of her made his pulse race.

He laughed at himself. The funny thing was, as miserable as he was, having Jenna in his arms again had made his heart soar. Slade thought back to the night he and Jenna had spent alone in her hotel room. When he considered it could be just one of many nights if she did become his girl, he couldn't feel happier.

Slade wasn't so sure how the hell it had happened but Mustang was right about one thing—it was too late now because he was good and caught, hogtied by one little city girl.

Chapter Twenty-Six

Jenna held her breath as Mustang lowered himself onto the bull's back. After seeing Slade dragged and trampled last competition, she'd barely been able to watch the other riders without feeling her heart race and having her stomach twist with worry. It had been difficult enough watching the strangers, even worse watching Chase and now Mustang, guys she actually knew and cared about.

Mustang nodded and the gate swung open.

Somehow eight seconds seemed to take an eternity. Watching Mustang's shoulder hit the dirt just after the buzzer sounded had Jenna covering her mouth to keep from crying aloud. Seeing him jump right up and scramble away from the charging bull nearly stopped her heart. When he high-fived the other guys down in the arena as the crowd cheered, Jenna's eyes misted with relief.

Then before she knew it, before she barely had a chance to recover from the stress of Mustang's ride, Slade was in the chute and the horrible anticipation started all over again. She'd have to remember to pack some antacids in her purse before the next night's competition because this worrying was going to give her an ulcer.

But Slade rode like he'd been doing it his entire life. The buzzer sounded and, in what seemed like slow motion, Slade released his hand from the rope and jumped to the ground, landing on his feet almost gracefully in a dismount that was the exact opposite of Mustang's messy tumble. She didn't care how pretty either of them got off the bull, as long as they were both off and safe.

One more guy rode after Slade, though Jenna couldn't tell you if he made the buzzer or not, and then it was over for the night. The riders would be back the following evening and, if all went well tonight with Slade and Mustang, Jenna too would be back to watch them.

Judging from the warm reception in the hallway, they were as happy to see her as she was to see them. That moment, with both of them there holding her, had dispelled nearly twenty-four hours of worry and doubt that mailing them her book would send them running in the opposite direction.

Maybe they didn't read it.

Jenna's heart kicked into overdrive as that thought struck. She let out a long, slow breath and tried to steady herself. If they hadn't read it yet, maybe she could steal it back from their hotel room. Sure, she could do that. Good plan. It might just work.

The plotting of her heist was interrupted by Mustang.

"Ready, darlin'?"

She glanced guiltily up at him. "Yup. Where's Slade?"

"He's just signing some autographs over there, but I figured I'd come collect you so when he's done we can take right off." Mustang's eyes twinkled and Jenna knew he was thinking way past their taking off, probably all the way to them taking off their clothes in the hotel room.

She was in perfect agreement with Mustang. Jenna's gaze sought the object of her desire, but when she found Slade she stopped dead in her tracks.

Mustang's hand touched her arm. "What's wrong?"

She realized her mouth was hanging wide open and shut it so she could answer. "There seems to be a bimbo attached to Slade's lips."

Jenna's words may have sounded like a joke, but the nausea rapidly growing in her belly at the sight of Slade kissing another woman was no funny matter.

Mustang spun to see what Jenna was talking about and laughed. "She's just some random fan, Jenna. That shit happens all the time."

"It does?" She kept her eyes on Slade as he grabbed the woman by the wrists and took a giant step back and away from her mouth. Jenna felt marginally better, but not much.

"Yeah, I had to sign the front of one woman's T-shirt before, while she was wearing it, which was preferable actually because I had to sign one girl's naked boob once."

Jenna scowled. "Yeah, I'm sure you hated that a lot."

"It's all nothing to worry about, darlin'. Believe me. I like a woman who offers a bit more of a challenge." He ran his hand up and down her arm.

She didn't like the turn of the conversation one bit, but at least Slade had extricated himself from the tart and was heading their way.

When he arrived, Slade took one look at Jenna's face and frowned. "What's wrong?"

As if he didn't know. Jenna screwed up her mouth in what she was sure was a very unattractive pout but she really didn't care.

"She's pissed about that fan...you know...kissing you." Mustang hooked a thumb in the direction where Slade had been molested.

Slade dipped his head once in Jenna's direction. "I don't blame her. I was pretty pissed myself. Girl thinks she can just go around kissing anyone she likes."

He knocked his hat back angrily and Jenna smiled, relieved. "Come on, let's go."

"Sounds like a plan." Mustang grinned and continued to do so as they crossed the street, entered the lobby and rode the elevator. He smiled right up until the three of them were standing in front of the hotel room door, and then he hovered at the doorway. "You know, I think I'm gonna run down to the store and pick us up some beer and snacks."

Slade narrowed his gaze at Mustang. "You could have thought of that while we were all downstairs."

"Well I didn't, now did I?" Mustang met Slade's glare with a look of schooled innocence and then addressed Jenna. "I'll be back in a bit, darlin'."

He dropped a quick kiss on Jenna and sprinted for the elevator. Turning back, Jenna saw Slade shaking his head.

"What's wrong?"

"He needs beer and snacks like he needs a hole in his head."

Jenna frowned and looked down the hall just in time to see Mustang disappear through the elevator doors. They slid shut behind him with a whisper and she heard the car rattle in the shaft. "What was that all about?"

Slade's lips curled with displeasure. "Mustang thinks we need some time alone."

He opened the door with his keycard, reached in and flipped on the light. While still standing in the hall, Slade swung the door wide with one arm so Jenna could enter the room before him.

She walked in then spun back to him. "Why should we be alone?"

"To talk." Slade made a face. He acted like Mustang had handed him a plate of raw liver to eat rather than a chance to be alone with her to talk.

"Okay." Jenna perched on the edge of the chair in the room. "We can do that. What would you like to talk about?"

Slade leaned against the bureau and folded his arms across his chest. "Um, I read your book."

Ah. Things were beginning to make sense.

Jenna's nerves kicked into high gear. "And?"

"It was good. Real good."

"I wasn't looking for compliments. What did you think of the story?"

Slade smiled. "You used what I told you about my first bull ride."

"Yeah. I did." *Almost word for word.* Jenna cringed. "Was that okay? It was just so beautiful... I'm sorry."

He held up a hand. "It's okay. I don't mind. It was kind of flattering actually. It didn't hurt that the girl gets so turned on by it in the story that she jumps him."

Cheeks heating, Jenna nodded. "Yeah. That is kind of how it happened in real life too."

Slade let out a short laugh. "Yeah. I remember. In fact, I haven't forgotten a thing. Not one minute of the time we spent together."

Jenna's entire body reacted to that proclamation. Warming. Melting. "Me neither."

He smiled. "Yeah, you even wrote it all down."

"It was wrong of me not to ask you permission first..."

"No, that's not what I'm getting at, Jenna. Besides, you changed our names. It's not like anyone will know."

She nodded, not mentioning that should Chase ever get a hold of the book, he would know she was writing about Slade and Mustang. But Jenna really hoped that should that happen, Chase would believe all the sexual escapades were created out of her imagination and not recorded from reality.

"What I'm trying to say is... What I'm asking is... The woman in the book, she falls for the two cowboys, pretty hard actually."

Jenna swallowed hard. "Yes."

Slade draw in a big breath then let it out slowly. "Then I guess my question is, do you picture us, the three of us, I mean, ending up like that?"

"Can I ask you a question first?"

"Um, sure."

"In the book, the cowboys fall for the girl too."

Slade nodded. "Yup. They do."

"And? Do you feel that way about me?"

Kicking at the carpet with the toe of his cowboy boot, Slade finally wrestled his eyes up. "Um, I guess you could say that, yeah."

Shaking, Jenna rose from the chair and moved toward him. "Really?"

Slade took a step forward, putting him a breath away from her. He tipped his head down so she could feel the warmth of his words. "Yeah. Really."

Jenna swallowed. "Then I guess I should tell you that in my first draft I had her choose only one cowboy, but my critique partner said it would sell better if they all ended up together."

She watched his eyes open slightly wider at that. His hands rose to grip her shoulders and Jenna thought she saw insecurity shining through a crack in his hard facade. "Which one did you pick...did she pick? In your first draft, I mean."

"The heroine chose the cowboy who made her fall in love with him with that story about his first bull ride."

Slade's eyes spoke everything he was feeling, even though he said only one word. "Good."

Then his lips were upon hers, his mouth hot when his tongue sought hers. His hands roamed her body like he was trying to memorize every inch of her. Her hands did the same, missing him all over again after the months they'd spent apart.

"I want you to be mine, Jenna. I mean really mine. I know it will be tough long distance, but maybe I can visit between competitions, and maybe you can come see me too."

"We can make it work, but you're going to have to get a cell phone," she warned.

Slade smiled. "Okay. Deal."

Jenna nodded then she pulled away, frowning. "Will Mustang be okay with you and me, you know, being a couple?"

"He knows how I feel." Slade laughed. "Mustang knew long before I did, or at least before I was willing to admit it."

"He did leave us alone to talk."

"There's something else we have to talk about. Mustang...he expects to come back here and—" he motioned to the bed, "—you know."

"Is that what you want?" Jenna liked Mustang, a lot, but she was in love with Slade.

"I think that's up to you." Slade watched her closely, his face suddenly a closed book once more.

"I know you share a lot—" If that's what it took for them to be together, then that's what she'd do.

"Jenna, I would be very happy to never share you again with another living soul. Hell, I'd be even happier if I could legally beat the crap out of every man who ever even looks at you."

She laughed as her heart did a little tumble. No man had ever wanted to beat anyone up on her behalf before. "Okay."

Slade's face remained stoic. "But I want you to know this. I will do anything it takes to keep you in my life and if you want...if what you need..."

"What are you trying to get at, Slade?"

He let out a sigh. "I'm saying I know you enjoy being with Mustang, and if it means I have to share you with him once in a while, on occasion, rather than lose you completely, I'm willing to give it a try."

Jenna smiled. How silly they both were, wanting each other, wondering what the other one was thinking, making assumptions. Slade's fears were the same as her own. "That is quite an offer, Slade."

He nodded solemnly. "Yup."

Slade's concession was both magnanimous and insanely intriguing at the same time. "You'd be willing to do that for me even though you'd rather beat him up for just looking at me?"

He dipped his head again. "Yup."

There was the man of few words she'd fallen in love with. Jenna leaned in to him and rose up on tiptoe. "Don't get scared, but I think I love you, Slade Bower."

"I've never said those words before, Jenna. Maybe to my mama, but not like that to a woman."

Cat Johnson

Jenna drew in a deep breath, resigning herself after his confession that she wouldn't be hearing them now.

His grip tightened on her arms. "I never said it because I never felt it. But I'm pretty sure I feel it now with you." He laughed. "Wow. Saying that wasn't as hard as I thought it would be."

Jenna laughed too. "I'm glad, because it shouldn't be hard, Slade."

The hotel phone ringing interrupted the kiss Slade had been about to deliver. With a deep sigh, he released his grasp on her and answered it.

"Hello?" He listened for a second and then covered the mouthpiece. "It's Mustang. He says some of the guys are going out and he needs to know if he should go with them or come back here."

The question hung heavily in the air between them, but the answer was clear to her. It had been clear for quite a while now. Jenna liked Mustang, but she loved Slade. She was a one-man woman after all.

"Tell him that as a native New Yorker, I suggest he go out and enjoy the city. Just be careful."

The look of resignation on Slade's face disappeared as he broke out into a huge smile. He relayed the message, hung up the phone afterward and came back to her. "So, does that mean the answer to the sharing question is no?"

Jenna nodded and Slade's hands rewarded her by taking a journey down her back to settle on her butt.

"For tonight, anyway." Slade frowned and she laughed at him. "Hey. What woman would totally close the door on an offer to have two cowboys dedicated to pleasing her in bed?"

Slade's eyes narrowed. "You've been writing too many of those naughty romance books, woman."

234

"I'm just teasing you, but you should thank God I did write that book. It's what brought us together."

"Yes it did and for that I'll always have a special place in my heart for naughty romance books."

"And for naughty romance-novel authors?"

Slade smiled. "Just the one."

Jenna smiled too, happier than ever. "Good."

About the Author

As an award-winning author of contemporary erotic romance in genres including military, cowboy, ménage and paranormal, Cat Johnson uses her computer so much she wore the letters off the keyboard within a year. She is known for her creative marketing and research practices. Consequently, Cat owns an entire collection of camouflage shoes for book signings and a fair number of her consultants wear combat and cowboy boots for a living. In her real life, she's been a marketing manager, professional harpist, bartender, tour guide, radio show host, Junior League president, sponsor of a bull-riding rodeo cowboy, wife and avid animal lover.

To learn more about Cat Johnson, please visit www.catjohnson.net. Send an email to cat at catjohnson.net or join her MySpace at www.myspace.com/authorcatjohnson or her Facebook at www.facebook.com/authorcatjohnson. Follow Cat on Twitter at www.twitter.com/cat_johnson.

The heart wants what it wants…

Rough Stock
© 2009 Cat Johnson

Bronc riders Mason and Clay have shared both good times and bad as best friends, but they never expected to share their boss's daughter, April. Can two friends love one woman, body and soul, without it destroying them?

The heart wants what it wants. For April that means not choosing between the two cowboys she loves, no matter how wrong it may seem inviting them both into her bed.

Life sends the three lovers in opposite directions, but a devastating injury brings them all together again. Their relationship now is no less bittersweet—or complicated—than before. Once severed, old ties leave scars that are tough to heal…

Warning: When you choose a man who thinks 8 seconds is a long time, perhaps you need two of them. In other words: Watch out, this book contains hot ménage sex with two cowboys and the woman they love.

Available now in ebook and print from Samhain Publishing.

Some things are worth playing for keeps.

Playing for Keeps
© 2009 Shiloh Walker

Jacob has always been part of Dana Cochran's life. They've lived next door to each other for years, they've dated on and off and now they see each other through work. But their timing has just never been right, and when Dana invites Jacob over to *play* with her and Mason Caldwell...things get complicated.

Doctor Jacob McCoy loves Dana. So much so, that he's even willing to share her with Mason Caldwell. But a red-hot threesome isn't all that Jacob wants from Dana.

When tragedy strikes their fledging relationship, Jacob has to convince Dana that pushing him away isn't the answer. He wants to be in her life forever. And some things are worth fighting for.

Warning: This title contains scenes of a woman being made very happy by two hot men, and enough emotion to have you reaching for the Kleenex.

Available now in ebook from Samhain Publishing.

LaVergne, TN USA
19 October 2010
201375LV00003B/1/P